A STORMY NIGHT
IN TOKYO

JASON J. HAYWARD

Dedicated to...

Mom – No matter what. No matter when. You have always been there for me and I love you.

Sydney – Thank you so much for all of your help and input. Without it, this book would not have been possible.

CONTENTS

CHAPTER ONE

A Chance Encounter

R ain hammered against the gleaming windows of the towering office building, creating a blurry veil over Tokyo's normally vibrant lights. The wrath of nature was in stark contrast to the imposing glass facade of Tokyo Gaming, which defied the storm with some of its lights still aglow.

Within its reflective walls, the hallowed boardroom was the stage for an intense drama. At the center stood Akiko Kimura, CEO of Tokyo Gaming. While she embodied grace and sophistication in her sharp business attire, the barrage of questions from the executive team conveyed tension in the room.

"Why were last quarter's projections off by such a huge margin?" one executive asked.

"With no warning or explanation about the shortfall?" demanded another.

Despite the relentless grilling, Akiko maintained a calm demeanor. Under that calm surface though, she felt as though she were being crushed alive.

As the meeting drew to a close, the executives left the room one by one, eventually leaving Akiko alone. She returned to her office, which was a private sanctuary filled with awards, framed accolades, and personal memorabilia. Closing the door behind her, she let out a sigh as her facade crumbled and tears filled her eyes.

It was late in the night now, and Tokyo's streets were mostly empty. During the meeting, the skies above Tokyo had opened up and begun hammering the city with relentless rain. Akiko, desperate to escape the oppressive atmosphere of the office, decided to head home. As she stepped outside, she found herself under the overhang of the massive building, sheltered, but just out of reach for any passing cabs to notice her. At least she was out of the rain.

A short distance away, Jake Rossdale, with his rugged good looks and a demeanor that hinted at an American upbringing, leaned against the building's wall. The glow from his cigarette momentarily illuminated his face each time he took a drag. He was in the process of lighting another cigarette when he noticed Akiko's futile attempts to hail a cab. As she stepped into the rain, he sprang into action.

Taking swift strides, he grabbed his umbrella, opened it, and in one smooth motion, stood beside Akiko, sheltering her from the torrential downpour. Instinctively, he raised his hand to hail a passing cab.

She looked at him, her face a mixture of surprise and gratitude. But then, regaining her poise, she remarked, "You really shouldn't smoke. It makes you smell terrible."

Caught off guard, Jake simply stared into her eyes, captivated. With their eyes still locked, he took the umbrella and gently put it in her hand. Softly, he wrapped her fingers around the handle. Akiko stood, looking at Jake with a mixture of confusion and sweet appreciation. As the cab pulls to the curb, she opens the door and starts to step in. She moves to hand Jake back the umbrella.

"Keep it," he said, his voice soft and caring. "I want you to stay dry when you get back out."

"Do you work in this building?" Akiko asked, a hint of recognition flickering in her eyes.

"Yeah, for Tokyo Gaming. Which means I work for you I guess?" he replied with a slight grin.

Akiko's eyes softened as she gave him a small smile. "Thank you for the umbrella. I will return this tomorrow. Apologies for the smoking comment. That was rude. It's been a long day." And with that, she was whisked away into the stormy night.

Jake watched the cab disappear into the rain-soaked streets. He then made his way back inside, the dim lights of the empty office space guiding him to his modest cubicle. He settled into his chair, lost in a maze of thoughts of the mysterious CEO he had just encountered.

When Akiko reached her high-rise condo, the rain continued to dance against the windows, creating a rhythmic patter. The room was dimly lit, with a warm amber glow coming from carefully placed fixtures. Everything in her living space spoke of wealth, taste, and meticulous selection. However, the vastness of the condo and its elegant decor couldn't hide the stark emptiness.

Akiko slowly shed her business attire and traded it for something more comfortable. Her fingers lingered on the umbrella as she placed it on the counter. It was just an umbrella — an ordinary object. But its presence and the memory of how it came to be in her possession evoked a warmth in her. The image of Jake hurrying toward her and shielding her from the rain, played in her mind. His unexpected act of kindness had been a silver lining on an otherwise horrible day. Somehow, she felt an undercurrent of connection with him.

Meanwhile, back at the office, Jake's curiosity got the better of him. Having never been to the executive suites before, he was somewhat mesmerized. The plush carpets, ornate artwork on the walls, and the serene ambiance were a stark contrast to the cubicle maze he was accustomed to.

As he walked down the hallway, he felt an odd mixture of awe and trepidation. He noted the names on the doors as he passed and wondered about the people who sat behind them. But there was one name he was especially curious about.

Reaching the end of the corridor, he hesitated for a moment outside Akiko's office. Taking a deep breath, he gently pushed the door open, and the room revealed itself to him. A large mahogany desk sat in the center and was surrounded by shelves filled with books, awards, and a few personal photos. Everything in the room was beautiful, yet it felt... lonely. He had sought out her office to find a glimpse into her world. He succeeded.

The room was a testament to Akiko's success, but it also whispered of her sacrifices. Jake realized the weight of responsibility she carried, the challenges she faced, and perhaps the loneliness she felt at the top.

After a few minutes, a wave of self-awareness washed over him. This was not his world and not his place. With a final glance around the room, he decided to leave. He failed to notice, however, that he'd left the lights on, marking his presence for whoever would come next.

CHAPTER TWO

A Beautiful Memory

The rain continued to pound the city. Tokyo's streets glistened under the downpour, reflecting the urban lights in puddles and wet surfaces. The rhythmic sound of raindrops drumming on roofs and windows provided a calming backdrop to the otherwise bustling city.

Tucked away in a quiet corner of the city, a nondescript door led to a haven of warmth and the savory aroma of broth and cooked noodles. The wood-paneled interior of the ramen restaurant, with its dark, worn-out timber and soft lighting, exuded an old-world charm that was hard to find in the modern metropolis of Tokyo.

Jake pushed open the door, the little bell overhead jingling softly. The warmth enveloped him and immediately drove away the chill of the rain-soaked streets. His eyes quickly scanned the place before settling on a familiar face.

"Steven!" Jake exclaimed, his face lighting up.

Steven, with his tousled hair and casual attire, looked every bit the excited tourist. His eyes sparkled with the wonder and curiosity of someone experiencing Japan for the first time. Standing up, he embraced Jake in a tight hug.

"It's been way too long, man!" Steven said, his voice filled with genuine happiness.

Jake grinned. "You have no idea how good it is to see you!"

Taking their seats at the bar, they were greeted by the owner, an elderly man with gray hair and a gentle smile. Jake's regular visits had turned them into good acquaintances.

"Ah, Jake-san! The usual?" the owner asked in his deep, raspy voice.

Jake nodded. "Yes, please. And a beer. Sapporo."

While waiting for their ramen, Jake and Steven caught up on old times, reminiscing about their college days, past adventures, and mutual friends. Their conversation flowed easily and quickly moved from personal updates to Steven's impressions of Tokyo.

"You know, despite the skyscrapers and the neon lights, there's something timeless about this city," Steven mused, looking around the cozy restaurant.

Jake smiled. "Exactly why I fell in love with it."

As their bowls of ramen arrived, piping hot and brimming with delicious ingredients, the two friends dug in. The rich broth, tender meat, and perfectly cooked noodles were a testament to the chef's years of experience.

Between mouthfuls, Steven shared his plans for exploring Tokyo while Jake gave him tips and recommendations. The afternoon turned into a montage of shared laughter, stories, and the simple joy of reconnecting.

Outside, the rain continued its dance, but inside the ramen restaurant, time seemed to slow down. The past and present blurred, leaving Jake with a beautiful memory to cherish. The kind of memory that made rainy days in Tokyo feel magical.

The rustic warmth of the ramen restaurant contrasted sharply with the cool, damp air outside. Steven zipped up his jacket, a grin plastered on his face. "That was some of the best ramen I've ever had!"

Jake chuckled, "I told you. This place is a hidden gem."

As they walked through the rain, Steven's curiosity got the better of him. "So, what's your office like? I want to see where you work."

Jake shrugged. "It's not much, just a cubicle. But it's got a pretty decent view. We can swing by on the way to the movie."

The duo made their way to the Tokyo Gaming building. The rain seemed to make the skyscraper even more imposing with its glass facade reflecting the stormy gray of the sky.

Upon entering the building, they were greeted by the soft hum of lights and the quiet hush of an office on a weekend. Jake led Steven through a maze of corridors and cubicles.

"Here it is," Jake said, stopping in front of his cubicle. The workspace was modest and decorated with only a few personal items – a framed photo, some souvenirs from his travels, and a small potted plant. A large window next to his desk offered a sweeping view of the city.

Steven whistled. "This view is next level. I can see why you like it here."

Jake grinned and led Steven back to the elevator. "Yeah, it has its moments. Wait until you see it on a clear day."

The low hum of the office was broken only by the soft 'ding' of the elevator arriving. Jake and Steven were caught off-guard when the doors slid open to reveal Akiko. Time seemed to slow as their eyes met. The look of surprise on her face mirrored Jake's own and the unexpectedness of the encounter heightened the tension of the moment.

As Jake looked at Akiko, she asked, "Are you...coming in?"

With a nervous chuckle, Jake entered the elevator followed by Steven. Nervously, Jake looked straight forward but stole the occasional glance at Akiko. Steven watched with a silent curiosity.

Jake had grown used to seeing Akiko in her sharp, business attire.

The casual outfit she had on now painted her in a different light. She was more relatable and human. The backpack she carried suggested she'd perhaps been to the gym or was running errands. Her tennis shoes were a sharp contrast from the elegant heels that normally graced her feet. It was a side of Akiko Jake hadn't seen before, and it intrigued him.

The silence in the elevator was palpable, punctuated only by the soft hum of its machinery. Jake found himself fumbling for words but couldn't find any. Steven, picking up on the subtle dynamics at play, chose to remain silent, though his eyes darted between his friend and Akiko with a mix of curiosity and amusement.

Akiko's voice, when she finally spoke, was soft and polite. "Are you having a nice weekend?" she asked, more to fill the silence than to actually inquire.

Jake gave a sheepish grin. "Yeah. We just had lunch. Going to see a movie now."

The three of them stood in the confined space, each seemingly lost in their own world. The air was thick with unsaid words and unacknowledged feelings. Jake and Akiko exchanged fleeting glances and their eyes communicated a depth of emotion words couldn't capture.

When the elevator dinged again, signaling its arrival at the Executive Floor, Akiko gracefully stepped out. She paused for a brief moment, her gaze settling on Jake. "Have a nice weekend, Jake. I will return your umbrella on Monday." Her voice was soft but firm.

Jake nodded as he raised his hand a bit. "Ah, no worries. Please keep it, Ms. Kimura."

She turned and walked away, leaving Jake and Steven in the elevator. Before the doors closed, she stopped and looked back with a warm look in her eyes. "Call me Akiko?." The doors closed, and Jake and Steven looked at each other. A startled look was on Jake's face.

Steven finally broke the silence by raising an eyebrow playfully. "So… you and Akiko, huh? She's cute."

Jake groaned and leaned against the elevator wall. "No. Not even close."

Steven smirked as he joked, "Please, call me Akiko I will return your umbrella?"

Shaking his head, Jake laughed. "Come on, let's go."

As the elevator descended, Jake couldn't help but replay the brief, unexpected encounter in his mind. The weekend had just begun, and already it had presented a memory he wasn't likely to forget.

The cinema was a kaleidoscope of colors, sounds, and emotions. The silver screen dominated the dark room, its images casting a soft glow upon the rapt faces of the audience. The latest action blockbuster from Hollywood had drawn a full house, and the room buzzed with anticipation.

Steven, like most of the audience, was engrossed in the movie. Each explosion, chase scene, and dramatic reveal had him on the edge of his seat. His eyes never left the screen, and occasionally, he'd lean over to whisper excitedly to Jake about a particular scene or plot twist.

Jake, however, was miles away. Every few minutes, his gaze would drift from the screen to an empty point in the darkness. The vibrant visuals, intense sound effects, and dramatic score failed to hold his attention. His mind kept drifting back to the unexpected elevator encounter with Akiko.

The memory played over and over in his mind - the surprise in her eyes, the softness of her casual attire, the way she'd said his name. Each detail was vivid, making the movie in front of him a pale comparison to the real-life drama he was experiencing.

At one point, a romantic scene played out on the screen. The lead characters shared a passionate embrace, and their chemistry was palpable. Jake felt a pang in his heart. He imagined himself in a similar scene with Akiko, their emotions laid bare without the barriers of corporate hierarchy and professional decorums to satisfy.

He was pulled from his reverie by a nudge from Steven. "Hey, you okay? You've been zoning out," Steven whispered, concern evident in his eyes.

Jake forced a smile. "Yeah, just a bit tired. It was a long week."

Steven studied his friend for a moment and then nodded, turning his attention back to the movie. But he made a mental note to check in with Jake later. It was clear that something, or someone, was weighing on his friend's mind.

As the credits rolled and the lights in the theater slowly brightened, Jake felt a mix of relief and regret. Relief that he could escape the confining space that amplified his feelings, and regrets that he hadn't been fully present with Steven.

They exited the theater and the cacophony of Tokyo's streets greeted them once more. Steven, ever observant, decided it was time to address the elephant in the room. "All right, out with it," he said, looking Jake squarely in the eye. "What's going on?"

Jake hesitated for a moment before letting out a sigh. "It's... complicated." He knew he couldn't avoid the conversation for long. But for now, the rain-soaked streets of Tokyo offered a welcome distraction.

High above the city streets, the view from Akiko's office was breathtaking. Tokyo's sprawling skyline stretched out in every direction, its myriad of buildings shimmering under the rain's gentle touch. But on this day, the beauty outside failed to capture Akiko's attention.

She sat behind her large mahogany desk, paperwork spread out in organized chaos, and her laptop opened with a plethora of unread emails. But her thoughts were elsewhere, and her heart felt an unfamiliar heaviness.

With a frustrated sigh, Akiko pushed back her chair and stood up to stretch her tense muscles. She wandered over to the massive window, her reflection ghostly translucent against the gray backdrop of the stormy city. In the reflection, her eyes betrayed her; they were lost, searching for something – or someone.

Jake's image flashed before her, a memory of their short encounter in the elevator. It was a mere moment, yet it left an indelible mark on her. The brief shared glances, the palpable tension, and the unspoken words lingered and pulled at her heartstrings.

Making a sudden decision, Akiko left her office and headed to the elevators. She felt an inexplicable urge to connect with Jake, or at least with the world he inhabited in the company. It was irrational, perhaps even unprofessional, but she couldn't resist the pull.

The doors of the elevator slid open, revealing the vast expanse of cubicles that made up Jake's floor. It was deserted, save for the muted hum of computers and the soft flickering of overhead lights. Akiko wandered between the rows, her tennis shoes pressing softly against the floor, the subtle sound echoing in the stillness.

Finding Jake's cubicle, she paused. His workspace was neat, with a few personal touches. A framed photo of a younger Jake with a group of friends, a small potted plant, and a mug with the inscription 'World's Okayest Employee'. Akiko couldn't help but smile at that. She took out her phone, snapped a photo of the picture on Jake's desk, and gave a guilty smile.

She lingered, her fingers tracing the edge of his desk as she took in the small details that painted a picture of the man she barely knew, yet felt inexplicably drawn to. The weight of their unspoken connection felt almost tangible in the stillness of the cubicle.

With a soft sigh, Akiko left Jake's cubicle and made her way back to the elevator, hoping that Monday would provide some answers to the whirlwind of emotions she was feeling.

As she returned to her office, the city lights had started to come alive and were painting Tokyo in a myriad of colors. But inside, Akiko felt a mix of hope, confusion, and anticipation. The weekend couldn't end soon enough.

CHAPTER THREE

Pictures of You

In the heart of Tokyo's bustling nightlife district, the club was alive with energy. Vibrant beats reverberated throughout the venue, dictating the rhythm of swaying bodies. Neon lights painted the crowd and created a dazzling play of colors and movement. Along the bar, people chatted comfortably, their laughter piercing through the music.

Steven was deeply engrossed in conversation with Ayumi, a local he'd met at the club. Their interaction was light-hearted and easy-going, their mutual interest evident. Around them, the world seemed to blur, leaving just their shared space.

Adjacent to them, Jake was noticeably distant. Yuki, a woman with raven-black hair and captivating hazel eyes, tried her best to engage him. Yet, Jake's polite responses and distracted demeanor signaled that his attention was elsewhere.

Growing curious, Jake pulled out his phone and navigated to his company's website. His focus narrowed to one particular page: Akiko's professional headshot. Poised and confident, her image seemed to draw him in, offering a contrast to the lively atmosphere of the club.

Trying to regain his attention, Yuki playfully took his phone. "Who's this?" she inquired, pointing to Akiko's image.

Caught off-guard, Jake replied, "Oh, nothing. Just work."

Seeing his reaction, Yuki remarked playfully, "Someone is working overtime."

Jake simply smiled. Silently, he longed to be with Akiko. Even if it was just standing under the overhang in the rain two nights prior.

As the evening progressed, the club's atmosphere grew more electric. Steven and Ayumi seemed to bond over shared stories and jokes, while Jake's thoughts remained firmly anchored to the image on his phone and the tantalizing memory of Akiko under the umbrella.

The club's name, "Neon Dreams," seemed fitting. For Jake, the night was not about the dazzling lights or the music, but about introspection and a growing curiosity about Akiko. He felt the beginning of a new chapter unfolding with Akiko intriguingly at its heart.

In an upscale district of Tokyo, Akiko's condominium stood tall against the city's silhouette. A sophisticated blend of traditional Japanese aesthetics and modern design, her home was a reflection of her life – meticulously curated, successful, but perhaps, a touch lonely.

The dining area was set impeccably. Silverware gleamed in the dim light, and a gourmet meal was presented with the kind of precision only a top-tier chef could achieve. The dishes – an assortment of sashimi, grilled fish, tempura, and a delicate miso soup – sent fragrant wafts throughout the room. Yet, for all its appeal, the food remained largely untouched.

The rhythmic pitter-patter of the rain outside created a soothing background score and added to the evening's contemplative mood. Lost in thought, Akiko reached for her phone, her fingers quickly navigating to a picture she had taken earlier that day. It was a candid shot of Jake, perhaps during a lighter moment with his friends, where his genuine smile was captured.

Holding the phone closer, Akiko's gaze was fixed on the image.

Jake's presence in her life had been unexpected, and their brief interactions were filled with an unspoken understanding – a connection that neither had anticipated.

Taking a moment, she put the phone down and leaned back in her chair. The solitude of her surroundings became more palpable. The opulence of her home and the success she had achieved, all felt somewhat hollow in that quiet moment. A simple gesture, a brief encounter with someone like Jake, had the power to evoke feelings and reflections she hadn't entertained in years.

The evening wore on and the city outside her window pulsated with life. People were probably out, dancing, laughing, and living. While Akiko sat alone in her beautiful home, she felt strangely connected to the world, thanks to the unexpected bond she had started to form with Jake. As she sat, her thoughts drifted back to that night, sharing the umbrella, gazing into each other's eyes.

CHAPTER FOUR
Monday

Monday mornings in Tokyo Gaming's headquarters were typically accompanied by a bustling energy. The hum of conversation, keystrokes, and the frequent ping of incoming emails created a symphony of productivity. In his modestly-sized cubicle, Jake was in his element. He was deep in concentration as he navigated through layers of coding for the latest game in development.

Around him, his coworkers were engrossed in their tasks, but Jake's world had narrowed down to the lines of code on his dual monitors. He was on the brink of solving a particularly tricky issue when a subtle movement at the periphery of his vision made him glance up.

Walking gracefully through the maze of cubicles was Akiko. It was unusual for her to be down on this floor. Usually surrounded by an entourage of assistants or team leads, she was more commonly spotted in the glass-paneled meeting rooms or her spacious office upstairs.

Today was different. She was alone, her presence undemanding yet undeniably magnetic. Jake noticed she was dressed in a sharp business suit and her hair was pulled back in a neat bun. The soft lighting above her made her seem almost ethereal.

Their eyes met, and for a split second, the world faded away. She acknowledged him with a reserved yet unmistakably warm smile. Jake, momentarily taken aback, returned the gesture with a nod and a soft smile of his own.

She continued her walk, briefly pausing to chat with a few employees or make notes of things on her tablet. The entire floor seemed to respond to her presence. Conversations softened and postures straightened. It was evident she commanded immense respect, not just as the CEO, but as a leader who was genuinely interested in the well-being of her team.

When she left the area, Jake found himself replaying the brief interaction in his head. Her smile, genuine and unexpected, had set the tone for his week. Monday, usually a day of routine and predictable patterns, had just become a lot more interesting.

The plush carpeting of the executive suite muffled Jake's steps, making him feel even more conspicuous in the quiet hallway. Each door bore a nameplate that was polished and elegant. They announced their occupants in both English and Japanese.

Takeshi Masuda's door was slightly ajar, the golden lettering on the glass reading 'Vice President of Marketing'. Taking a deep breath, Jake knocked softly. A voice from within beckoned him in.

The office was large, adorned with art that showcased Japan's rich history and its modern advancements. Behind a grand mahogany desk sat Masuda, a man in his early fifties. His sharp features softened with the hint of a smile. "Rossdale-san, this is unexpected," he remarked, observing Jake with a curious eye.

Jake straightened up, trying to gather his thoughts. "Thank you for seeing me, Masuda-san. I know this isn't usual protocol, but I have some ideas for our upcoming game's marketing campaign that I hoped would be valuable."

Masuda leaned back, genuinely intrigued. "It's not every day a programmer ventures in here with marketing suggestions. But I am all ears." They chatted for a while, Jake pitching his concepts with passion, and Masuda listening attentively, occasionally nodding or asking questions.

As the conversation drew to a close, Masuda offered, "While marketing isn't your primary role, Rossdale-san, it's clear you have some good ideas. I wish others on my team had the same passion for storytelling... and this game, that you do."

Buoyed by the unexpectedly positive meeting, Jake thanked him and stepped out into the corridor. But as he made his way back to the elevators, he happened to glance toward one of the glass-walled conference rooms. Inside was Akiko, surrounded by charts and executives. She was mid-discussion and her focus seemingly intense.

But as he passed by, their eyes locked. There was a fleeting moment of surprise on her face followed by that unmistakable warmth Jake had come to recognize. It was clear she was attempting to maintain her professional demeanor, yet the corners of her eyes crinkled ever so slightly and hinted at her restrained smile. Jake responded with a subtle nod, his heart rate slightly elevated.

As the elevator doors closed to take Jake back to his floor, the brief but loaded exchange replayed in his mind. The boundaries of their professional lives were beginning to blur, and the impending adventure promised to be anything but routine.

The sun had already begun its descent and was painting the Tokyo skyline in a fiery embrace of orange and pink. Tokyo Gaming's glass façade reflected this twilight tapestry, making the edifice seem like a glowing beacon amidst the city's vast expanse.

Exiting the building, Jake felt the cool evening air on his face, a refreshing contrast to the controlled environment of the office. Instinctively, his eyes traveled upward, searching the matrix of windows to pinpoint Akiko's office. He knew it was a pointless gesture, but some part of him hoped to catch a fleeting glimpse of her silhouette against the radiant backdrop.

He stood there for what felt like minutes but were mere seconds torn between the urge to stay and the rationale to move on. He chose the latter. Taking a deep breath and walking away, he immersed himself in the sea of people navigating Tokyo's intricate sidewalks.

Little did he know, but mere moments after he disappeared from view, a figure appeared by one of the windows high above. It was Akiko. She had just wrapped up her meeting and, on an impulse, had walked over to the window, perhaps prompted by the same indescribable pull Jake had felt earlier.

She scanned the street below, a touch of disappointment clouding her eyes as she failed to spot the familiar figure she was subconsciously hoping to see. There was a hint of wistfulness in her gaze as she watched the bustling streets and thought about the multitude of stories they carried and the one that had been silently unfolding between her and Jake.

Shaking her head softly as if to clear her thoughts, she turned back to her desk. But as she started packing her belongings, her fingers lingered on a small photograph of a recent company event. There, amidst the crowd, was Jake, his face animated in conversation. Akiko smiled a mix of melancholy and hope as she placed the photograph back. She made a silent promise to herself to embrace the unfolding narrative with both its uncertainties and its potential.

CHAPTER FIVE
Aikido

The dojo had an air of stillness that belied the intense energy of the few practitioners who trained there. Polished wooden floors gleamed, reflecting the soft overhead lights, which in turn illuminated the training mats and the shoji screens lining the walls.

Jake, dressed in his black gi, moved fluidly across the mats, his body twisting, turning, and executing a series of throws and locks with an intensity that was palpable. Each movement, steeped in years of training, was delivered with precision and purpose. His uke – the person on the receiving end of the techniques – had difficulty keeping up, such was Jake's newfound fervor.

Off to the side, Ichikawa-san, the dojo's sensei, observed with a sharp eye. He was a lean man in his late sixties with lean silver hair and lines etched deep into his face that showed his years of discipline and understanding of the depths of martial artistry. His gaze was fixed on Jake, noting not just the physical technique but the emotional energy driving it.

When Jake paused to catch his breath and wipe sweat from his brow, Ichikawa-san approached, his footsteps silent on the dojo floor.

"You are like a storm today," Ichikawa remarked, a hint of admiration in his tone. "It's been a long while since I've seen you harness such intensity, Jake-san."

Jake bowed slightly, acknowledging his sensei's words. "Thank you, Ichikawa Sensei. I... I've had a lot on my mind recently."

Ichikawa-san's eyes, always perceptive, searched Jake's. "Aikido is not just about physical balance but emotional balance too. Whatever is occupying your mind is also fueling your spirit in training."

Jake looked down and considered his words. "Yes, Sensei. Life outside the dojo has been... interesting."

Ichikawa-san gave a small nod. "Life often is. But remember, the principles of Aikido don't only apply here. Blend with the situation. Don't fight against it. Redirect the energy. And most importantly, find your center. In life, as in Aikido, balance is key."

Jake took a deep breath and absorbed the wisdom. "Thank you, Sensei. I'll remember that."

The two exchanged bows of respect, and Jake returned to his training, the words of his sensei echoing in his mind, guiding his movements, and providing a clarity he hadn't realized he'd been seeking.

Jake slid his feet into his shoes and felt the weight of his Aikido gi in his duffel bag. The dojo was quiet now, save for a few students conversing in hushed voices.

"Jake-san," a voice resonated, causing Jake to turn. Taka Hojo stood a few feet away, his posture upright and demeanor commanding respect. His once-inked arms were a testament to his past, a past that he had left behind but still bore the scars of. The Yakuza tattoos peeked out from under the sleeves of his crisp white shirt. Taka's transformation from a Yakuza member to an Aikido practitioner was the stuff of legends in the dojo. It was a story of redemption and self-discovery.

"Good evening, Taka-san," Jake greeted, bowing slightly.

"I was watching your practice today," Taka began, his voice gravelly.

"Very impressive."

Jake smiled, slightly embarrassed. "Thank you. I had some... motivations."

Taka nodded, a knowing look in his eyes. "Sometimes, that is all we need. Motivation to push us and to help us discover what we are truly made of." He paused for a moment, then asked, "Have you eaten?"

Jake shook his head. "Not yet."

Taka gestured towards the exit. "Join me for dinner? There's a place not far from here. They serve the best tonkotsu ramen."

Jake hesitated for a moment, then nodded. "Sure, sounds great."

The two men left the dojo together, walking side by side through the bustling streets of Tokyo. The neon lights reflected off the wet pavement and painted a vivid picture of the city's nightlife.

Taka led Jake to a small ramen shop that was nestled between two larger buildings. The warm glow from inside spilled onto the street. Once inside, the aroma of simmering broth filled their senses.

The two men took a seat at the counter and ordered bowls of ramen and some sake. As they waited, Taka looked over at Jake, his expression serious. "Jake-san, life has a funny way of presenting us with challenges. But it is how we face them and how we let them mold us, that defines our path."

Jake pondered the statement while swirling the sake in his cup. "I've been facing a few challenges of my own lately."

Taka nodded. "Life outside the dojo can be as much of a battleground as inside it. Remember to find your center."

Their food arrived, and the conversation shifted to lighter topics. Still, Taka's words resonated with Jake. By the end of the night, Jake not only had a renewed perspective on his current situation, but he also found an unexpected mentor in Taka Hojo.

The clinking of ceramic bowls and muted conversations filled the small ramen shop. Jake took a sip of his sake and let the warmth spread through him. He cast a side glance at Taka, contemplating. "Taka-san," he began hesitantly, "we've known each other for years now, practiced side by side, but this... tonight, it's the first time we've ever gone out like this. Why now?"

Taka placed his chopsticks on the bowl and wiped his mouth with a napkin. He took a moment before speaking and appeared to be choosing his words carefully. "Jake-san, when I first joined the dojo, the whispers were loud. I felt eyes on me, judging me for the life I had lived, and the tattoos that marked my skin. But you." Taka pointed at Jake. "You did not turn away. Instead, you welcomed me. You treated me as an equal, not as an outsider."

Jake shrugged, a bit taken aback. "Everyone has a past, Taka-san. Who am I to judge? What matters is the present and the choices we make now."

Taka smiled faintly. "Your perspective is rare, Jake-san. But it's why I respect you. You saw past the exterior and the rumors. You saw a man trying to change and find a new path. For that, I am grateful."

Jake leaned back, swirling the sake in his cup. "I never thought much of it. I saw someone passionate about Aikido and someone willing to commit and learn. I wanted to call you a friend."

Taka's stern face softened. "And I am honored to be called that. Our paths crossed for a reason. Perhaps the universe saw two souls needing companionship, guidance, and understanding."

Jake raised his cup. "To new beginnings and old friendships."

Taka clinked his cup with Jake's. "To the journey ahead."

As the night deepened and the ramen shop began to clear out, Jake and Taka continued their conversations, exploring topics beyond the dojo. It was the beginning of a deeper bond, a bond forged out of mutual respect and understanding.

Jake, curious about Taka's past, ventured a question. "Taka-san, I hope this isn't too forward, but why did you leave the Yakuza? What made you change your path?"

Taka looked deep into Jake's eyes, a glint of a shadowed past visible for a fleeting moment. He took a deep breath, then simply said, "Jake-san, that's a story for another time. I hope you can respect that."

Jake nodded understandingly. "Of course, Taka-san. Everyone has their reasons. I get that."

Taka smiled in appreciation. "Thank you for understanding. And to answer your next question, yes, I'll be at training tomorrow evening. I find solace and purpose in the dojo, and I am not ready to let that go."

Jake chuckled, "Neither am I. See you on the mat then."

As they prepared to leave, the chef approached them and bowed politely. "Tonight's meal is on the house," he said, glancing briefly at Taka.

Taka bowed his head in gratitude. "Thank you, Kuro-san. Your food, as always, is a gift."

Jake, sensing the underlying respect and unspoken history between the two men, simply smiled and joined in with a polite bow. "Arigatou, Kuro-san."

The two men walked out of the restaurant, the quiet camaraderie between them palpable. They parted ways at the corner, each heading to their respective homes, but with a newfound appreciation for the bonds that life unexpectedly creates.

The next night dojo was quiet, save for the soft rustling of a few students practicing their katas in the corner. Jake made his way to the private chambers at the back where Sensei Ichikawa often did his administrative work after classes. Pausing at the door, he knocked gently.

The door slid open to reveal the venerable face of Ichikawa-san, his eyes always seemingly looking beyond what was in front of him. "Jake-san, is everything okay??"

Taking a deep breath, Jake voiced his thoughts. "Sensei, I've been pondering my path and purpose here in Japan. I was wondering if, in time and with the right training, I could ever be considered for an instructor's position here?"

Ichikawa looked at him thoughtfully. "Jake-san, you have always been a dedicated student, but recently, I have seen a change in your intensity. A new fire. What has brought about this shift?"

Jake hesitated for a moment, searching for the right words. "Japan, Sensei, has become more than just a temporary residence for me. It's become... home. And I want to contribute to the community that has given me so much. I want to put down roots. Real roots."

Ichikawa took a moment to ponder this, then nodded slowly. "Your dedication is impressive, Jake-san. However, being an instructor requires more than skill. It requires a deep understanding of our culture, traditions, and philosophy. Are you prepared for that?"

Jake nodded firmly. "I am, Sensei. I'm willing to learn and put in the effort."

Ichikawa smiled gently. "Then, Jake-san, we shall see what the future holds. Dedication and time will tell."

Jake bowed deeply, gratitude evident in his eyes. "Thank you, Sensei."

As he left the dojo that evening, Jake felt a renewed sense of purpose. He was ready to embrace his future in Japan with all the challenges and rewards it promised.

CHAPTER SIX
Dinner Date

The soft, neon glow of Tokyo's evening streets enveloped Jake as he wandered past the formidable Tokyo Gaming building. Looking up, he spotted Akiko's office light still on. Concerned she might be skipping dinner due to her workload, an idea sprung to mind.

A nearby restaurant, its aroma tantalizing passersby, seemed like the perfect place. Though Jake had never been, he'd heard coworkers praise its dishes. Deciding to surprise Akiko, he stepped in and ordered a popular dish to go, ensuring it would stay warm.

With the aromatic package in hand, he made his way back to Tokyo Gaming, his heart pounding in anticipation. Riding the elevator up, he mentally rehearsed how he'd present the meal to her. However, upon reaching her office, his plans quickly unraveled.

Peering through the slightly ajar door, he saw Akiko deep in conversation with a man he didn't recognize. Their conversation seemed intense and earnest. Akiko looked up at that moment and her eyes locked with Jake's. The recognition in her eyes as she saw the restaurant bag was immediate. Her face mirrored a mix of surprise and gratitude.

But Jake, seeing the unfamiliar man and not wanting to create an awkward situation, shifted his gaze downward. Clutching the bag tighter, he quickly turned and left, retreating to the elevator.

All he felt as the elevator doors closed behind him was the weight of the missed opportunity.

The office's ambient light dimmed, signaling the late hour. Akiko stretched her back, looking around her office and out at the sprawling city lights. The past few hours had been filled with strategizing and negotiations that left her mentally exhausted. The man she had been meeting with was an important client from overseas and discussions had run much longer than anticipated.

Shaking off her fatigue, her thoughts quickly turned to Jake. The image of him standing outside her door with a restaurant bag in hand played in her mind. She realized his intention and it warmed her heart. Even after hours, he'd been thoughtful enough to bring her food.

She briskly walked toward the elevators, hoping she might still catch Jake in his cubicle. The soft hum of the office's nightly operations echoed as she navigated the maze of desks, but Jake's area was empty. The only illumination came from a single desk lamp and his screensaver that cast a soft glow over a few scattered papers.

Drawn to his workspace, she noticed the pictures and trinkets that gave a glimpse into Jake's life. Wanting to leave a sign of her gratitude, she rummaged through her bag for a pen. Finding one along with a post-it, she scribbled a quick "thank you" not punctuating it with a heart symbol and her initials "A.K."

Placing it prominently in the center of his keyboard, she hoped it'd be the first thing he'd see come morning. With a sigh, she turned, heading back to her office, the weight of the day catching up to her, but with a newfound appreciation for the small gestures that can brighten one's day.

Chapter Seven

Going Back to Cali

Jake's footsteps echoed softly in the nearly empty corridors of the Tokyo Gaming offices as he arrived early, eager to start the day. The dim morning light painted a soft hue over the room, filtering through the glass windows. The tranquil atmosphere, however, was immediately interrupted when his gaze fell upon the neatly placed post-it note on his desk.

His heart skipped a beat as he read Akiko's handwriting – a simple "thank you" with a heart symbol, and her initials. He could almost hear her voice and the delicate timbre of it in those words. A gentle smile graced his face as he delicately took the note and placed it into his wallet, a small keepsake to remind him of the undeniable connection he felt with her.

Jake took a deep breath and got ready to begin the day's work. He switched on his computer. The hum of the machine filled the room, followed by the familiar chime indicating it was ready. He quickly opened his email and prepared himself for the deluge of messages that awaited.

However, his focus narrowed on a bolded, unread email from his supervisor. Jake's eyes scanned the contents, and he sat up straighter. The company wanted him to fly to Los Angeles for some meetings at the American offices. The prospect of leaving Japan, even temporarily, filled him with a mix of emotions: excitement about returning to his home city of L.A. but also dread at the inevitable distance from Akiko.

Taking a moment, he leaned back in his chair and stared at the sprawling cityscape outside. Tokyo''s early morning beauty offered a calming influence. He then started drafting a reply, confirming his availability for the trip and assuring his supervisor he'd be prepared.

As he finished the email, Jake wondered if he should mention this to Akiko. Would she miss him? He shook off the thought, reminding himself not to get ahead of things.

However, as the day progressed, the thought of the impending trip and the distance from Akiko stayed at the forefront of his mind. He was already missing her in advance.

The city's hustle and bustle was a stark contrast to the peace inside the Tokyo Gaming office. Yet, amidst the noise and activity, Jake's thoughts were dominated by a single idea – ensuring Akiko knew how much their growing bond meant to him before he left for LA.

Just as Jake was about to compose a message to Akiko, suggesting they meet for coffee, his supervisor, Mr. Tanaka, approached his cubicle. The older man's normally calm demeanor seemed a bit hurried today, his brow slightly furrowed.

"Jake," Mr. Tanaka began, looking around as if ensuring they weren't being overheard. "There's been a change of plans. You need to leave for Los Angeles tonight. Your flight is at midnight."

Jake blinked in surprise. "Tonight? I thought…"

Mr. Tanaka ran a hand through his hair. "I know, and I apologize for the sudden change. There's been an urgent development and they need our best on the ground there. That's you, Jake."

Jake hesitated for a moment, thinking about the whirlwind of emotions he was feeling regarding Akiko. However, he knew the company relied on him, and he couldn't let them down. "All right," he replied, nodding slowly. "I'll head home and pack up."

"I appreciate it." Mr. Tanaka said and patted Jake on the shoulder appreciatively. "I trust you'll represent us well. Safe travels."

Jake gave a half-smile. "Thanks Tanaka-san."

With the urgency of the situation, Jake quickly logged off from his computer, grabbed his belongings, and headed toward the elevator. He felt a tug in his heart as he realized he wouldn't be able to have that coffee with Akiko and share the news. He wanted, more than anything, to see her one last time before his trip.

As he reached the ground floor and made his way to the building's exit, he paused and looked back up. The urge to run back and find Akiko was overwhelming. However, he reminded himself that he had responsibilities. Taking out his phone, he quickly composed a message to Akiko:

"Hey Akiko, unexpected change of plans. I'm heading to LA tonight for some urgent meetings. Wanted to see you before I left, but time's not on my side. Let's catch up when I get back. Take care."

With that, he hesitated, took another look at the message, and deleted it. He knew all too well that all emails were tracked by Human Resources and did not want to make any waves. He had another idea.

Later that night, while making his way back through the familiar streets near their offices, he couldn't shake the thought of Akiko. It felt important, somehow vital, to let her know in person about his sudden trip. Texts and emails felt too impersonal for the connection they had begun to forge. So, despite the ticking clock, Jake found himself walking back toward the Tokyo Gaming offices.

He swiped his access card and entered the dimly lit office space. Most of the cubicles were empty at this hour. The hum of the air conditioning was the only sound punctuating the otherwise quiet night. He made his way to the executive suite, hoping to catch Akiko before she left.

However, as he approached her office, he noticed the light was off. That was unusual; Akiko often worked late, just like him. A sinking feeling took hold along with the realization that he'd missed her.

He stood for a moment outside her office and weighed his options. Eventually, he stepped inside. The serene ambiance of her space always had a calming effect on him. He spotted a blank piece of paper on her immaculate desk. Borrowing her pen, he quickly jotted down, "Had to go to LA last minute. Let me know if you need anything." Wanting to add a touch of warmth and personal sentiment, he sketched a simple flower next to his note.

As he set down the pen, he felt a mixture of satisfaction and regret. Satisfied because he had, in his own way, tried to reach out and make a personal connection, and regret because he wouldn't see her smile, hear her voice, or experience any reaction she might have upon reading his message.

With the note left on her desk as a silent testament to his thoughts, Jake made his way out of the office. Each step took him further away from Tokyo and closer to the next phase of his journey. The streets outside seemed more vibrant and were filled with the life and hustle of the evening crowd, yet Jake felt a touch distant. He already was feeling the space of the miles that would soon separate him from this place and Akiko.

Boarding a taxi, he directed the driver to the airport. As the city lights passed by in a blur, Jake leaned back and tried to find solace in the rhythm of the journey. His thoughts lingered on the unexpected turns life often throws one's way.

As the queue for boarding slowly dwindled, Jake took the moment to gaze out of the large windows overlooking the runway. The faint hum of airplane engines in the distance mixed with the chatter of passengers, announcements, and the sound of luggage wheels on the polished floor. Though he had taken many flights before, there was a certain unease tonight and a weight in his chest that he couldn't place.

Suddenly, the serene melody of his phone's ringtone broke his trance. Quickly fishing it out of his pocket, he glanced at the incoming call display. An unfamiliar Japanese number flashed across the screen. A hopeful thought crossed his mind - could it be Akiko?

Without hesitation, he swiped to answer. "Hello?"

"Jake-san," a familiar male voice greeted him. It was not Akiko, but his supervisor from the Tokyo Gaming offices. The slight disappointment was hard to mask, but Jake kept his composure. "Just wanted to remind you to keep us updated about the progress of the meetings in LA. The higher-ups are quite keen to know how things are going."

"Of course, I'll ensure you're in the loop," Jake replied and glanced ahead as the line shortened.

"Safe travels, Jake-san," the supervisor added before ending the call.

Slipping the phone back into his pocket, Jake stepped forward. As he handed over his boarding pass, he glanced one last time back at the terminal. A silent wish echoed in his heart that he could share this journey and this experience, with someone special.

Settling into his seat, he allowed the ambient noise of the cabin to lull him into a state of reflection. As the plane took off and soared into the darkness, Jake felt both the thrill of a new adventure and the tug of what he was leaving behind. The twinkling city lights of Tokyo faded below him, and as they did, the face of Akiko filled his thoughts, a beacon of warmth in the vast expanse of his mind.

The gentle hum of the airplane's engines, combined with the subtle sway of the aircraft made it feel like Jake was being cradled in the arms of a giant. An overhead light cast a dim glow on his reclined seat, and a soft snore occasionally escaped his lips.

The plane was quiet, with only a few passengers moving about. Some were reading, some were working on their laptops, and most, like Jake, were deep in sleep. The flight attendants moved with practiced silence, ensuring the comfort of their passengers.

Suddenly, the stillness was broken by a gentle chime. The seatbelt sign illuminated, and a soft voice came over the intercom, "Ladies and gentlemen, we're experiencing some minor turbulence. We ask that you please return to your seats and fasten your seatbelts."

Jake stirred, momentarily disoriented. He reached for the blanket draped over him, pulling it tight. As the plane rocked gently, memories seeped into his half-awake state. Fragments of conversations, moments shared, and the image of Akiko's face all flashed before him.

The airplane jolted slightly, waking Jake fully. He tightened his grip on the armrests, his thoughts now consumed by the present moment. The turbulence continued for several minutes before the plane stabilized, and the seatbelt sign was turned off.

Exhaling a deep breath, Jake closed his eyes once more. This time, though, sleep eluded him. He thought of the times he had spent with Akiko, their shared moments, and the unspoken emotions between them. The distance between Tokyo and Los Angeles felt so vast, and he felt an overwhelming longing to bridge that gap.

A flight attendant approached and offered a drink. "Would you like something to help you sleep?" she asked, her voice soft.

Jake hesitated for a moment, then replied, "A Diet Coke, please?"

As he sipped the cool liquid, he looked out of the window. An ocean of darkness lay below, which was dotted with occasional lights from ships or distant cities. He thought about the meetings awaiting him in

LA and the challenges they presented. But for now, those concerns took a backseat to his thoughts of Akiko. As dawn approached, Jake finally drifted back into a restless sleep. His dreams were filled with familiar faces and memories of Tokyo.

CHAPTER EIGHT
Los Angeles

The metallic screech of the plane's tires hitting the tarmac jolted Jake from his half-awake state. As the plane taxied to its gate, the familiar sights and sounds of LAX enveloped him. The bright California sun streamed through the windows, and Jake could hear the distant hum of traffic and the city's hustle beyond the airport's confines.

As Jake stepped off the plane, the dry Los Angeles air greeted him. The city was both familiar and foreign all at once. The scents, the sounds, and the pace of life - everything felt amplified and overwhelming in a way he hadn't anticipated.

He made his way through the terminal past billboards advertising the latest Hollywood blockbusters and tourists excitedly chatting about their vacation plans. Overhead, announcements echoed in various languages, reflecting the melting pot that was Los Angeles.

While waiting at baggage claim, he felt a peculiar sensation. Here he was, in a place that had once been home, yet he felt like a stranger, an outsider. Japan had changed him more than he had realized.

Once he collected his luggage, Jake hailed a taxi. The city sprawled out before him as they made their way to his hotel in downtown LA. Buildings rose into the sky, their glass facades reflecting the golden sunlight. The streets were lined with palm trees, and people bustled about, everyone seemingly in a rush.

Jake checked into his hotel, a modern skyscraper with views of the sprawling city below. As he unpacked, he glanced at his phone and noticed a few unread messages. One from Steven, checking in on him, and another from his supervisor, detailing the upcoming meetings.

Jake's thoughts drifted to Akiko. He wondered how she was, and what she might be doing at that very moment. He considered reaching out to her but hesitated because he was unsure of what to say. They seemed to have a connection, but he couldn't rush it. He had to play it cool.

That evening, he ventured out into the city. The bright lights of downtown LA danced before his eyes, and the night was alive with energy. As he walked along the streets, memories flooded back. He recalled his college days, nights out with friends, and the dreams he had chased when he first moved to LA.

Stopping at a street-side food truck, he ordered some tacos, a taste he had missed while in Japan. The sizzle of the meat and the spicy aroma was all so nostalgically delicious.

While savoring his meal, Jake's mind wandered to the differences between his two worlds: Tokyo's hustle and elegance and LA's vivacity. He pondered the delicate balance between his past and present and between the life he once knew and the one he had come to cherish in Japan.

As the night deepened and LA's skyline sparkled, Jake felt a tug in his heart. He knew he had important meetings to attend and responsibilities to uphold. But more than anything, he yearned for the comfort of Tokyo and the chance to see Akiko once more.

After settling into his hotel room and absorbing the atmosphere of the bustling city outside, Jake felt a pang of homesickness. Not for Tokyo, but for the California coast and the warmth of his childhood home.

Realizing he hadn't spoken to his parents in a while, he decided to give them a call.

Picking up his phone, he dialed his mother's number. It took only a few rings before her voice answered. It was filled with surprise and joy. "Jake? Is that you?"

"Hey, Mom," Jake replied with a chuckle. "It's been too long."

"Oh, sweetie, it has! How's Tokyo? Are you still enjoying it there?"

Jake paused and searched for the right words. "Tokyo is amazing, Mom. But I'm actually in LA right now. Just landed today for some work meetings."

There was a brief silence on the other end before his mother exclaimed, "You're in LA? And you didn't tell me?"

Jake sighed. "I know, I know. It was a last-minute trip. I'm here for just a week or so, but I wanted to see if I could come by and visit before heading back."

"Oh, Jake, of course! Your father and I would love to see you. When can you come?"

Jake looked at his schedule. His days were filled with meetings, presentations, and networking events. "I'm tied up for most of the week, but I can make a trip to Malibu this weekend. Would that work?"

"That's perfect. We'll have a family dinner, just like in the old times. And bring any laundry you have; you know I like to take care of my boy," she said with a touch of playfulness.

Jake laughed. "Sounds perfect, Mom. I've missed you guys."

"We've missed you too, sweetie," she replied, her voice filled with warmth. "Drive safe when you come, and call if you need anything."

"I will, Mom. Love you."

"Love you too, Jake."

Jake hung up the phone and felt a weight lifted off his shoulders.

The idea of seeing his parents, being surrounded by the familiar settings of his childhood, and the salty air of Malibu brought comfort to his heart. As excited as he was about his life in Tokyo and the burgeoning feelings for Akiko, he realized how much he still cherished the ties to his home in California. The duality of his life - the interplay between his past in Malibu and his present in Tokyo - was something he continued to grapple with. But for now, he took solace in the fact that he would soon be surrounded by the love and warmth of his family.

The hustle and bustle of the Los Angeles office was a stark contrast to Jake's tranquil Tokyo workspace. Due to the high ceilings and open floor plan, the murmur of activity constantly echoed throughout the vast expanse of the building. The walls were adorned with posters that showcased the latest gaming sensations, and there was a palpable energy that was distinctively American.

Jake took a moment to absorb his surroundings as he was ushered into a large, modern conference room. The room was filled with colleagues, some of whom he recognized from his earlier days with the company, while others were fresh faces. They greeted him with friendly nods and warm smiles and acknowledged his journey from Tokyo.

As he settled into a chair, a sleek presentation began to play on the large screen at the front of the room. Graphics and statistics flitted across the screen, demonstrating the company's current market performance and projections. The lights dimmed slightly, and Jake felt the weight of his jet lag pressing down on him.

His eyes darted from slide to slide as he attempted to maintain focus. The room's temperature seemed just a tad too warm, and it was lulling him into a drowsy state. The presenter's voice, while articulate and engaging, began to take on a droning quality in Jake's ears. He could feel his eyelids becoming heavy, and every few minutes, he would shake his head slightly, trying to fight off the wave of fatigue threatening to overtake him.

During a brief coffee break, Jake splashed cold water on his face in the restroom. He looked at his reflection and noted the bags under his eyes. "Just a few more hours," he told himself.

Returning to the conference room, he decided to engage more actively by asking questions and providing insights from his experience in the Tokyo market. This active participation seemed to help, but he could still feel the lingering effects of the time difference.

As the day wore on, Jake's internal clock wreaked havoc on his concentration. While others debated strategies and evaluated potential risks, his mind would occasionally drift to thoughts of Tokyo, the bustling streets, the serene temples, and, inevitably, Akiko.

The meetings finally came to an end in the late afternoon. Exhausted but satisfied, Jake left the office, and the LA sun greeted him with a warm embrace. Thinking of Akiko, he relaxed in the taxi as they headed back to his hotel.

The plush bed in Jake's hotel room beckoned. The crisp white sheets and the softness promised a brief respite from the day's exhaustion. But as he began to drift off, the familiar chime of his cell phone jolted him back to reality.

Squinting at the screen, Jake saw his mother's name displayed. "Hey, Mom," he greeted, trying to mask the weariness in his voice.

"Jakey!" his mother exclaimed, her voice bubbling with excitement. "Your dad and I were thinking. Now that you're back, even if just for a short time, why not have dinner together tonight?"

Jake hesitated, the weight of his jet lag pulling at him. The idea of a comforting family dinner was enticing, but he wasn't sure he could muster the energy. However, hearing the hope in his mother's voice, he couldn't refuse. "Of course, Mom. It sounds great. Do you want to come to the hotel?"

"Yes, dear. They have that lovely restaurant on the ground floor, don't they? Let's meet there at 7:30."

"Sounds like a plan. I'll see you then."

Hanging up, Jake set an alarm on his phone to give himself a short power nap. Within seconds, he was sound asleep.

Jake was awakened by the shrill sound of his alarm. Groggily, he checked the time; it was already 7:10 pm. He quickly freshened up, changed into a more casual outfit, and made his way downstairs.

The hotel's restaurant was bathed in a soft amber glow, and the clinking of glasses and the hum of conversation created a warm ambiance. As Jake entered, he spotted his parents seated at a table near the window. His mother's eyes lit up when she saw him, and his father stood to envelop Jake in a strong hug.

Dinner was a blur of laughter, stories, and shared memories. His parents regaled him with tales of their recent adventures while Jake shared some of his experiences in Japan. Though he was careful not to mention Akiko directly, he couldn't help but let her presence seep into some of his anecdotes.

His mother, ever observant, noticed the subtle changes in her son. "Someone in Japan has caught your eye, hasn't she?" she teased.

Caught off guard, Jake blushed. "Mom!"

His dad chuckled and gave him a knowing wink. "Your mother always knows."

As they waited for their starters, Jake's mom cleared her throat and her face adopted a more serious demeanor. "Jake," she began, "I've been meaning to talk to you about something."

Jake looked up, sensing the gravity in her tone. "What's up, Mom?"

She took a deep breath before continuing. "Samantha has been calling the house quite frequently. She's been asking about you and wondering how you're doing."

Jake blinked in surprise. Samantha was a name he hadn't heard in years and was a chapter he thought he'd closed before moving to Japan. "Really? After all this time?"

His mother nodded. "Yes, and she sounded sincere, Jake. She mentioned that she still has feelings for you and regrets how things ended between you two."

Jake's father, always the more reserved of the two, added, "We always thought she was a good match for you. Your mother and I believe it might be worth considering. Everyone makes mistakes."

Jake felt a twinge of annoyance. "I'm only back for a short while, Dad. I've built a life in Japan, and I have responsibilities there."

His mother's face softened, her eyes filled with concern. "I just want you to be happy, Jakey. And if there's a chance for you to find that happiness here, with someone who truly cares for you, wouldn't it be worth exploring?"

Jake sighed and ran a hand through his hair. The memories of Samantha and their relationship flooded back: the good times, the laughter, the arguments, and the eventual painful breakup. "Mom, it's complicated. I appreciate your concern, but I'm in a different place now."

His mother looked at him for a moment and studied his face. "I know she did wrong, but she knows what she lost."

Jake hesitated, then nodded. "What she did was horrible. And unforgivable. But I am glad she learned her lesson."

His parents exchanged glances. Jake's dad spoke up, "Then, hold strong."

Jake smiled weakly, grateful for his father's understanding. "Thanks,

Dad."

The conversation shifted to lighter topics as the evening wore on, but in the back of Jake's mind, he could not stop thinking of Akiko. His last relationship felt like a million years ago and he would never go back. His future was Akiko. He was certain.

CHAPTER NINE

Just a Glimpse

Jake's eyes were heavy, and he found himself struggling to focus on the presentation being given. The large conference room in the Los Angeles office was filled with a mix of familiar and unfamiliar faces. Soft murmurs filled the room as people whispered to one another and shared thoughts on the latest company strategies. The hum of the projector and the buzz of fluorescent lights seemed to amplify Jake's exhaustion.

For what felt like the hundredth time, he discreetly checked his watch, hoping that the meeting would draw to a close. Just as he was calculating how many hours he had left, the host, a tall, immaculately dressed woman named Marianne, introduced a new segment. "We'll now be connecting with our Tokyo office for a joint session," she announced.

The screen changed from the PowerPoint presentation to a live feed of the Tokyo office conference room. Jake immediately perked up. He recognized several of his colleagues and began nodding and smiling as he saw familiar faces. He searched for Akiko.

Then, Akiko appeared on screen. She looked as professional and poised as ever. She was wearing a sharp business suit that contrasted beautifully with her delicate features. Jake couldn't help but smile as he felt an unexpected surge of warmth seeing her, even if it was just through a video link.

Marianne took a moment to introduce everyone on the LA side to their Tokyo counterparts. When she mentioned Jake's name, Akiko's gaze shifted slightly as though she were searching for him amongst the sea of faces.

"Jake! I heard that you were in L.A. How was your flight?" Akiko asked, a genuine curiosity in her voice.

Caught slightly off guard, Jake cleared his throat. "Good. The jet lag is real, but I'm managing. It's great to see you."

A soft smile played on Akiko's lips. "I will be expecting a souvenir."

The rest of the meeting progressed with the Tokyo team providing updates on their end. As discussions went back and forth, Jake found himself frequently glancing at the video feed and being drawn to Akiko's expressions and reactions. Despite the miles between them, Jake felt a closeness to her. It was a small but reassuring reminder of the bond they shared.

By the time the meeting finally ended, Jake was both exhausted and energized. Exhausted from the travel and endless meetings, but energized by the unexpected connection he'd shared with Akiko. As he gathered his things and headed out of the conference room, he couldn't help but wonder if she missed him as much as he missed her.

The plush carpet of the hotel room muffled Jake's footsteps as he made his way to the bed. His body felt heavy with exhaustion, but his mind was racing. He thought the comfort of the bed would instantly lure him into a deep sleep, but instead, he found himself tossing and turning amidst the sheets. The dim glow from the city lights outside seeped through the gaps in the curtains, casting a soft ambient light across the room.

An hour went by, maybe two, and Jake realized he wasn't going to fall asleep anytime soon. The weight of the day's events, the encounter with Akiko over the video conference, and the reminders of his past from his mother's dinner conversation churned in his mind.

With a sigh, he sat up and slipped his feet into his shoes. He needed some fresh air.

Exiting the hotel, the LA evening greeted him with a gentle breeze. The streets were less crowded than during the day, but there was still a palpable energy. The City of Angels had a way of coming alive at night in a way that was entirely different from Tokyo.

Jake wandered aimlessly and let the streets guide him. He passed by neon-lit bars with thumping music, quiet cafes with a few patrons enjoying a late-night coffee, and street performers playing to the small crowds gathered around them.

As he walked, he found himself reflecting on his life in Japan and how different it was from his life in LA. He missed the hustle and bustle of Tokyo, the tranquility of the Aikido dojo, and, of course, his budding connection with Akiko.

He stopped at a square and found himself surrounded by skyscrapers. Jake pulled out his phone and found the picture of Akiko he'd taken from the company website. He looked at it for a moment, smiled, and began walking.

The neon lights of various shops illuminated the streets, drawing Jake in with the allure of LA-centric merchandise. Somewhere between his introspection and wandering, an idea had formed in Jake's mind. Wanting to bring a piece of LA back to Akiko, he decided to pick up some souvenirs. After all, she did say she was expecting something. Recalling her words brought a grin to his face. He was definitely bringing her something.

His first stop was a quirky boutique that had a window display adorned with vintage Californian memorabilia. Inside, he found a soft stuffed bear with a little surfboard and "LA" embroidered on its foot. He could imagine Akiko's face lighting up at the cute trinket, so he promptly added it to his purchases.

Next, he stumbled upon a street vendor selling custom apparel. He picked out a couple of hooded sweatshirts; one in a deep navy with a shimmering golden palm tree design and another in a soft gray, emblazoned with the iconic Hollywood sign. To complement the sweatshirts, he chose a baseball cap in a muted teal with an intricate "Los Angeles" stitched in white.

The final piece came from an artsy poster shop. The poster he chose depicted a painted LA skyline at sunset, with hues of purple, orange, and gold melting into each other and capturing the ethereal beauty of a city he once called home.

Returning to his hotel room, he laid out his finds on the bed and arranged them carefully to take a picture. The array of gifts felt like a bridge between his past in LA and his present in Tokyo, a fusion of two worlds he held dear. And he hoped that through these gifts, Akiko could feel a part of that connection.

Exhaustion finally catching up to him, Jake slid into bed and let the excitement of sharing these tokens of affection with Akiko lull him into a deep, restful sleep.

The Los Angeles office of Tokyo Gaming had a different vibe from the Tokyo branch. It was a sprawling open space with huge windows that let in an abundance of California sunshine, which warmed the wooden floor panels. Potted plants were scattered about, and the distant hum of the city outside gave it a pulse. Jake tried to settle into the rhythm of this place, despite the nagging jet lag and the events from the previous day.

His temporary desk was in a prime spot and gave him a panoramic view of both the interior of the office and the busy streets outside. But his brief respite was interrupted by Marianne, the stern-looking woman in her early 50s with silver streaks in her raven-black hair who managed the LA branch's operations.

"Jake," she called. Her voice carried a certain weight. "Can you come in here please?"

He stood up immediately and noted the urgency in her tone. As he entered the conference room, he noticed that it was filled with executive board members, and the room's atmosphere was heavy with tension. At the head of the table was the company's U.S. Operations Head, which Jake had only met once before.

"Good morning," Jake greeted, trying to sound as professional as possible.

"Morning, Jake," the Operations Head responded, giving him a nod. "Please, take a seat. We need to discuss something important."

As Jake took his seat, a screen came to life and began displaying graphs, metrics, and performance indicators. When Marianne began to speak, she explained the declining performance in certain markets and how crucial the next quarter would be for the company.

"We've been following the success of your projects in Tokyo, Jake," the Operations Head interrupted, his gaze fixed on him. "And we believe that you might be the right person to help us here in LA. You up for joining us here permanently?"

Jake was caught off guard. He had expected this trip to be a brief one where he simply offered insights from his Tokyo projects. But now, it seemed, they were considering a more permanent role for him in Los Angeles.

"We are not suggesting this lightly," Marianne added. "We think you have what it takes to turn things around here. We need leadership and dedication."

The weight of the situation pressed down on Jake. The allure of being back home, close to his family, with a significant promotion was tempting. But his life in Tokyo, the projects he had become so deeply involved in, and his budding relationship with Akiko anchored him there.

The meeting continued with Jake trying his best to absorb all the information. But in the back of his mind, a whirlwind of thoughts and emotions raged. He needed time to process and decide where his future truly lay. There was only one problem. He did not have time. They wanted an answer now.

Jake took a moment, allowing himself to breathe and collect his thoughts. He looked around the room, at the expectant faces of the executives and Marianne, then to the Operations Head who seemed to be scrutinizing him, searching for any hint of indecision.

"Thank you," Jake began, his voice measured and even. "I'm truly honored by the offer and the faith you have in me. It's not something I take lightly."

Marianne nodded, her stern demeanor softening ever so slightly. "We've seen the numbers from Tokyo, Jake. Your work is solid and you have the respect of your peers. We think that you are an excellent leader."

Jake took a deep breath. "I appreciate that, Marianne. But I've found a place in Tokyo. I'm invested in the projects there and I believe in what we're doing. And not just professionally," he added, thinking of Akiko and the intricate tapestry of relationships and experiences he'd woven into his life over the last five years.

The Operations Head leaned forward, interlacing his fingers. "Jake, this isn't just any promotion. It's a significant step up, both in responsibility and compensation."

Jake swallowed and felt the weight of the decision. But his resolve was unwavering. "I understand, sir. And I'm truly grateful. But my heart is in Tokyo right now. That's where I need to be."

A tense silence filled the room. Everyone seemed to be gauging Jake's determination.

The Operations Head finally broke the silence, "If that's your final decision, Jake…"

Jake nodded. "It is, sir. But I can't thank you enough for thinking of me."

The Operations Head sighed and a hint of disappointment in his eyes entered his eyes but also respect. "All right. I respect your choice. We'll arrange for your return to Tokyo. If you change your mind. Please let me know."

Jake felt a weight lift off his shoulders. He'd made the right decision for himself, even if it meant passing up a significant opportunity. As he left the conference room, he felt more certain than ever about his future in Tokyo.

CHAPTER TEN
Homecoming

The sprawling Los Angeles International Airport was bustling with activity as travelers rushed to catch their flights, bid goodbye to loved ones, or welcome them back. In a relatively quiet corner, Jake leaned against a pillar with his phone pressed against his ear.

"Mom, I'm really sorry," Jake began, trying to convey the genuineness of his apology. The weight of disappointment weighed on him even though he felt sure about his decision to head back.

His mother's soft voice, tinged with a hint of sadness, responded. "We were really looking forward to seeing you this weekend, Jake."

Jake sighed. "I know, and I wanted to as well. But something's come up at work. They want me back in Tokyo sooner."

His mother was silent for a moment. "It's that job, isn't it? Ever since you went to Tokyo, it's like we lost a part of you. Your dad and I just want you to be happy."

Jake's throat tightened. "I am happy, Mom. Tokyo feels like home now. But you and Dad will always be a part of me, no matter where I am. And you should come to visit."

He could almost visualize his mother's gentle smile. "I know, Jake. Just promise you'll come see us soon, all right?"

Jake nodded, even though she couldn't see him. "I promise. I'll find time soon."

After exchanging a few more words and assurances, they hung up. Jake looked at his boarding pass. The final call for his flight was announced.

As he stepped into the airplane, he felt a mix of emotions. The skyline of LA, the beaches of Malibu, and the familiar warmth of his parents all tugged at his heartstrings. But so did the neon lights of Tokyo, the bustle of Shibuya, the rhythm of his new life, and his budding feelings for Akiko.

The plane took off, and as LA receded into the distance, Jake's heart surged with anticipation. He was going home to Tokyo with a heart filled with hope and anticipation.

The ambient hum of Tokyo greeted Jake as he stepped off the plane. The fatigue from the whirlwind trip, coupled with the jet lag, settled heavily on him. Yet, something was energizing about being back. Tokyo had that effect on him. It was a city that was simultaneously chaotic and calming.

His taxi ride home was a blur and the neon lights of the city flashed by. As he neared his apartment, he noticed the gentle hues of the sunset painting the skyline shades of gold and pink that cast a warm glow on the busy streets.

Unlocking the door to his apartment, Jake was hit by a wave of familiarity. The faint scent of green tea, the soft hum of his air conditioner, and the pile of unread mail on his table – it was all so reassuringly mundane. He glanced at the bags of gifts he had brought for Akiko and smiled while thinking about the moment he'd hand them over to her.

But right now, all he wanted was to crash in bed. And that's precisely what he did. Kicking off his shoes, he didn't even bother changing out of his clothes before flopping onto his bed and pulling the comforter around him. Within seconds, he was in a deep, dreamless sleep.

Outside, Tokyo continued its rhythmic dance. Cars whizzed by and the distant sounds of the city lulled him further into slumber. The chapter in LA had closed, but a new one in Tokyo was just beginning.

The morning rays of sunshine filtered through the sheer curtains of Jake's apartment, kissing his face and rousing him from his sleep. There was a brief moment of disorientation as he tried to figure out whether he was in LA or Tokyo. The realization hit him - he was home. Tokyo was home now.

Stretching his limbs, Jake headed to the shower. The warm water cascaded down and washed away the remnants of his jet lag. As he dressed in his usual work attire, he couldn't help but glance at the bags of gifts he had set aside for Akiko. The urge to take them with him was strong, but he wanted the moment to be perfect. Not rushed. Not forced. So, he decided to leave them behind.

The streets of Tokyo bustled with energy. It was that same energy he had missed while in LA. He navigated his way through the crowds, picking up a fresh cup of matcha latte from his favorite stall while en route to the office.

The Tokyo Gaming offices loomed large as he approached. The familiar chime sounded as the glass doors slid open, and he stepped into the world that had become his daily life. Faces turned in his direction, and smiles were exchanged. The close-knit community of the office was evident as colleagues patted him on the back, inquired about his sudden trip to LA, and expressed their relief at his return.

"Jake! Good to see you back!" Hiroshi, one of the senior developers, exclaimed as he gave him a friendly slap on the shoulder.

His cubicle was untouched and looked just as he had left it. Setting his bag down, he powered up his computer. As he waited for it to boot up, he felt a presence by his side. Looking up, he found Akiko, her eyes filled with a mix of relief and curiosity.

"Welcome back, Jake," she greeted softly, a small smile playing on her lips.

The atmosphere in the room shifted slightly as if everyone sensed the unspoken bond growing between the two. They exchanged a few words and tried to catch up on what had been missed. It was simple, yet intimate.

The day had only just begun, but Jake felt invigorated. He was back where he belonged, surrounded by friends and colleagues who felt like family. Whatever lay ahead, he was ready to face it head-on.

In the sanctuary of his cubicle, Jake dove headfirst into his work. The screens in front of him were a mosaic of numbers, codes, and messages. There was a harmony in this organized chaos that he reveled in, each keystroke a part of the rhythm. Every so often, he'd pause, review the project updates, and adjust his plans accordingly.

Time seemed to blur, and the intensity with which he tackled his tasks left him in a zone. So engrossed was he that he barely noticed the shadows of people moving around him nor the general murmur of conversations that echoed in the expansive office space.

The gentle chime of a message notification broke his concentration. Looking at the bottom right corner of the screen, he saw a new message from Osamu: "Lunch?"

He replied with a quick affirmative and packed away his things. As he stood up, he stretched out the kinks in his back and neck from hours of focused work.

Walking down the open corridor, he met up with Osamu whose face bore the same traces of concentration that Jake's probably did. The two exchanged knowing looks, both aware of the workload and the necessity to occasionally escape from it.

When they exited the Tokyo Gaming building, the warm midday sun greeted them. The streets were alive with people moving to and fro as they sought out their favorite eateries or tried something new.

Osamu led the way to a cozy ramen place just a few blocks away. "It's new," Osamu explained, "Opened just the other day while you were in LA. I've heard good things."

Inside, the aroma was intoxicating – a blend of savory broth, fresh noodles, and tantalizing spices. They took their seats at the counter and placed their orders with the chef directly. While they waited, they caught up on the latest office gossip, discussed ongoing projects, and exchanged stories.

Jake recounted parts of his LA trip, mentioning the surprise meeting, the jet lag, and the whirlwind nature of the entire trip. Osamu listened attentively and offered his own tales of overseas adventures and the unique challenges they presented.

As their steaming bowls of ramen arrived, the conversation shifted from work to more personal matters, such as weekend plans, hobbies, and eventually, relationships.

"So," Osamu began, eyeing Jake seriously. "Akiko. Something I have to tell you."

Before Jake could speak, Osamu continued. "Don't pursue it. She has a boyfriend." Jake just looked at him, so Osamu continued. "He came back when you were in LA. He's an exec named Nobu. They went out the other night. I just don't want you getting blindsided."

Jake sat frozen. When he was finally able to respond, he said, "Wait, what?"

Osamu nodded. "People were talking. Sounds like you were... pursuing her. Just let it go, man. She's the CEO. No way that would have worked. She is kinda hot though."

All of a sudden, Tokyo disappeared and Jake felt more lost and alone than he had ever felt in his entire life. He looked at Osamu and had no idea how to respond.

Jake settled back into his workstation after the hearty lunch. The delicious ramen was now an added weight that made him feel even more lethargic. Still, deadlines loomed, and he tried to focus on the tasks at hand. He clicked through emails and worked on a few documents, but his concentration kept slipping and his thoughts returned to Akiko. Did he imagine it? Or was she just at his desk a couple of hours ago with that same beautiful look in her eyes?

A soft murmur of voices in the hallway caught his attention. Akiko's voice, unmistakably delicate and confident, floated toward him. Jake glanced up instinctively and searched for her familiar face. He caught a glimpse of her walking briskly alongside Nobu Fujitani. Nobu was the quintessential image of a modern Japanese businessman—sharp suit, gelled hair, and an aura of confidence.

Jake's eyes met Akiko's for just a fleeting second. There was a coldness, or perhaps just distraction, in her gaze. She didn't wave or even acknowledge him. It was as if their shared moments and their unspoken connection had vanished. Was this the effect of his unexpected trip to LA? Or had something changed while he was away?

Feeling a nudge on his arm, Jake looked to his right to find Osamu who had a forlorn look on his face. With a subtle raise of his eyebrows, Osamu wordlessly conveyed, "See? Didn't I warn you?"

Jake exhaled sharply, trying to shake off the unease that the encounter had stirred. He attempted to dive back into work, but the image of Akiko with Nobu and the coldness of her gaze refused to leave his mind.

The remainder of the day passed in a blur with Jake mechanically finishing his tasks. As the office began to empty, and the lights dimmed, Jake contemplated whether to talk to Akiko. Maybe it was just a bad day or perhaps there was more to the story.

He knew he couldn't let the uncertainty linger but choosing the right moment was crucial. And as the evening shadows lengthened, Jake made up his mind to find answers—soon.

CHAPTER ELEVEN

Aikido Therapy

The dojo was a place of serenity for Jake, a sanctuary where he had often found solace from the chaos of life. But today, his focus was scattered. Every move he executed lacked the precision and finesse he was known for. The graceful dance of Aikido, which had always been second nature to him, now felt awkward and forced.

Taka, observant as ever, noticed Jake's uncharacteristic fumbles. During one particular move, Jake's balance was so off that Taka easily overpowered him and sent Jake tumbling to the mat with a soft thud. This was unlike Jake, especially when paired with Taka. They'd always been equally matched and their bouts always ended in mutual respect and understanding.

Sensei Ichikawa was watching the session from the side and could see that Jake's mind was elsewhere. He motioned for the two to pause their sparring.

"Jake-san," Sensei began in his deep, measured tone. "Aikido is not just a physical act but a connection between mind, body, and spirit. Today, your spirit seems.. off. Remember, the battle within can be harder than any external opponent."

Jake sat up, sweat glistening on his forehead. "Apologies, Sensei. There's just... a lot on my mind tonight."

As Jake and Taka stepped out of the dojo, the night air was cool and carried the scents of the city. The streetlights overhead cast a soft yellow glow on the pavement, and the distant murmur of city life echoed around them. Taka leaned against the wall of the dojo, pulled a cigarette from his pocket, and lit it. He took a drag and the end glowed a bright orange in the dimness. He reached into his pocket, pulled out the pack of cigarettes, and nodded to Jake to see if he wanted one. Jake shook his head no.

"You know," Taka began, exhaling a stream of smoke upward, "an old Japanese says - 'To continue is power.' You can't just let things remain unsaid with her."

Jake shuffled his feet and looked down at the ground. "I know, It's just... complicated."

Taka smirked. "When is it ever simple? Look, from what you've told me, it seems you're reading a lot into things. You're crafting stories in your head based on snippets of information. But you won't find peace or clarity until you speak to her directly. The connection you feel is real, right?"

Jake sighed. "You're right. I've been avoiding the conversation because I'm scared of what I might find out. And yes, it is real. I just hope that has not changed."

Taka clapped him on the shoulder. "That's natural. But remember, no matter the outcome, it's better to know than to be in the dark. And whatever happens, you've got friends who have your back. Don't forget that."

Jake looked up and met Taka's earnest gaze. "Thanks, Taka. That means a lot."

Taka flicked his cigarette onto the street and crushed it with his heel. "Don't mention it. Now go and sort things out. Life's too short for maybes."

With a determined nod, Jake decided he would talk to Akiko the first chance he got. Whatever the outcome, he owed it to both of them to clear the air.

Jake paused on the busy streets of Tokyo, and his eyes were drawn to the lit window high atop the Tokyo Gaming offices – Akiko's office. The soft light from her room cast a gentle glow amidst the darkened surroundings of the building. Taking a deep breath, he mustered up the courage to confront the myriad of emotions that had been swirling inside of him for days.

He entered the building and the familiar hum of the central air conditioning and the faint aroma of green tea filled the air. Riding the elevator up, he went over the conversation he hoped to have in his head by rehearsing the words and anticipating Akiko's reactions.

The door to Akiko's office was slightly ajar when he arrived. Pushing it open slowly, he found the room bathed in a warm glow, stacks of paperwork on her desk, her computer still humming quietly, and an almost finished cup of tea that was still steaming slightly. To Jake, all of that indicated she had just been there. Yet, the room was empty. Akiko was nowhere to be found.

A feeling of frustration welled up inside of Jake. He had been so close to getting the answers he needed and the clarity he craved. He looked around hoping to find some hint of where she might have gone but there was nothing. He imagined her out at a romantic dinner, arm in arm with Nobu. The thought stung his heart and he pushed it away. Still, it lingered and gnawed at him.

With a heavy heart, he turned to leave. He would have to wait until tomorrow for answers. As he made his way back to his apartment, he rehearsed what he would say when he could finally look into her eyes and talk with her. The script playing over and over in his head.

The weight of the day's uncertainties pressed heavily on his mind. The apartment felt empty and slightly cold, much like the current state of his emotions regarding Akiko.

He carefully placed his backpack onto his bed and began to unpack some of the items from his recent trip. As he unfolded a Los Angeles hooded sweatshirt, he thought of how he had imagined giving it to Akiko and had even anticipated her reaction.

Lost in thought, he was startled when the doorbell echoed through his apartment. Jake's heart raced momentarily. Maybe she had finally decided to talk things through.

Hurrying to the door, he flung it open only to find Taka standing there. Jake blinked in surprise. It was unlike Taka to visit, especially unannounced. Taka's face bore a serious expression, and Jake could see a slight tension in his posture.

Jake looked at Taka with a mixture of surprise and disappointment. "Taka, you good?"

Taka nodded. "Yeah, I need a favor. I need you to keep this for me. Just for a few days."

Jake nodded and Taka handed him a backpack before continuing. "Don't look inside. I'll take good care of you. Just hold it for me, cool?"

Jake nodded again. Taka gave him a deadly serious look. "I owe you. I'll be back in a few days." Taka walked away quickly and Jake stood in the doorway for a few moments before going back inside.

Jake's head was now spinning. The emotional ups and downs of the day had hit him hard. He wanted to look in the bag but decided against it. After a moment of contemplation, he took the bag, slid it under his bed, and decided to leave it there until Taka returned to retrieve it. As Jake sat back down on the bed, he found himself concerned about what type of trouble his friend may be in and about the legality of holding that bag. Then, the doorbell rang again.

His mind raced. *"Taka's back already? Or worse, the Police?"*

He got up from the bed and made his way to the door. Cautiously, he opened it to find Akiko standing in his doorway with two hot Matcha green teas in her hands. Steam subtly rose from the cups. She smiled at him with undeniable chemistry. Jake stood frozen. A moment passed before he asked, "Akiko-san, what are you..doing here?"

She smiled. "May I come in?"

Jake snapped out of it and stepped back. "Yes, please come in. Of course."

As soon as she entered the apartment, she looked at Jake with an undeniable and uncharacteristic vulnerability. Jake stared back at her with a mixture of confusion and happiness. She smiled and handed Jake one of the cups. "Matcha green tea. Your favorite?"

He nodded yes as he accepted it. Akiko added, "Did I wake you? Do you have a moment to talk?"

Jake stammered slightly. "No, not at all. Yes, we can talk. For sure. Is everything okay?"

Akiko nodded. "Something happened. While you were in America..."

Jake looked down. He knew what was coming next. He couldn't look at her, so he just shook his head in a mixture of sadness and dejection. Akiko shook her head and proceeded, "People at work were talking about us. It got raised to me as an issue, and I had to do something."

Jake interrupted. "Your old boyfriend. The guy in the office today?"

She held up her hand. "No. He was never my boyfriend. I never felt anything for him."

Jake interrupted again with a hint of jealousy. "But you two were together, like in a relationship?"

Akiko sighed deeply. "It was a rough time in my life. I didn't know what I wanted and he was quite persistent."

Jake looked down at his feet unable to look her in the eyes.

Akiko continued. "Nobu was very helpful in my career. He is still on the board of directors. He can make things very difficult for me if he wants to."

Jake glared at her. "So, it's okay if you are with this Nobu guy? But not me?"

Akiko shook her head. "There are certain... allowances made for him. This felt like the best way to put the talk to rest. Nobody would question it."

Jake was hurt. He slowly pulled away from Akiko and made his way over to the bed where he picked up the bag of gifts he brought her from Los Angeles. He handed them to her silently. The look in his eye said everything. Akiko took hold of the bag and pulled out the stuffed animal. She smiled sweetly and an apologetic look floated onto her face.

Jake is unfazed. "I have been hurt before. Just not sure if I can do this. I hope you can understand."

Akiko nodded stoically and turned to leave. As they walk toward the front door of Jake's apartment, Jake asks, "Can I ask you something?"

She turned to face him. "Yes, anything."

He asked. "When I was in L.A., did you miss me?"

She paused for a long time before nodding yes and taking her phone out of her purse. She opened it and showed Jake the photo she took of the picture on his desk. He looked at the photo and back to her. He had no words. She proceeded by saying, "I went to your desk, looking for you. Missing you. I took this so I could feel you with me. Yes, Jake, I missed you. Terribly."

As Jake stood processing this, he took his phone out of his pocket, opened up the photos, and showed Akiko the press photo of her from the website. He added., "This photo of you. I have looked at it a thousand times. I memorized every line."

Tears welled up in Akiko's eyes. Jake reached up and wiped the tears away. She pulled in close and they embraced. She pulled back so Jake could see her face. Tears streamed down her beautiful, almost porcelain-looking face. "Jake, I have loved you since the very first time I looked into your eyes. When you gave me your umbrella and got me safely into the taxi and out of the rain."

Jake nodded and chuckled, "And you told me I smelled like an ashtray. I quit by the way."

She nodded. "I felt bad for saying that. I am not used to somebody taking care of me. And you didn't smell bad that night. I just didn't know what else to say."

The attraction between them was electric, but neither could make a move. Akiko continued, "If you can't be with me, I will understand. I will have to accept it. But I want you to know that you changed me, Jake. You made me feel again. You made me love. You made me love you. And I just want you to know that."

Jake chuckled. Not a funny sort of chuckle, but a chuckle that was a mix of relief and joy. "I love you too. I love you in a way that I never even thought possible. When I heard that you got together with... it just hurt."

She shook her head. "I would never. I only want you."

He smiled. "I only want you too."

Standing in the middle of Jake's apartment. The magical energy between them has returned. Akiko regained her composure. "Tomorrow is Friday. Do you have plans for this weekend?" Jake shook his head and

Akiko continued, "I have an idea. Meet me at Shinjuku Station, South West Entrance tomorrow at 7 p.m., okay?"

Jake's expression was a mix of surprise and intrigue. "I will be looking forward to it."

Akiko smiled, leaned in, and gave him a quick, sweet kiss, "Good night Jake, I love you. See you tomorrow. Shinjuku Station, South West at 7 p.m. Don't forget."

Akiko made her way to the door and exited into the night.

Jake stood at the door watching Akiko leave. He stood there for a full minute before closing the door and making his way back into the apartment.

CHAPTER TWELVE

Friday Night at Shinjuku Station

The neon lights of Shinjuku Station bathed the bustling area in a myriad of colors. The iconic electronic billboards advertising a plethora of products flickered and flashed, creating an almost hypnotic effect. It was the start of the weekend in Tokyo, and Shinjuku was alive with energy. People scurried about, each on their own journey.

Jake stood amidst this organized chaos and tried to take in the sights and sounds around him. He felt like a solitary figure in a constantly moving sea of humanity. His thoughts were still preoccupied with Akiko, Taka's visit, and the challenges at work.

Suddenly, a stranger approached him and began weaving his way through the crowd until he stood directly in front of Jake. The man was average in build with sharp, scrutinizing eyes. Dressed in a dark suit, he looked like any other businessman in the city, but there was an air of determination about him.

"You are Jake?" he asked, his voice clear and authoritative.

Jake, slightly taken aback, responded cautiously, "Yes, that's me. Can I help you?"

Without waiting for further acknowledgment, the man handed Jake a crisp, white envelope. Inside, Jake could feel the shape of a ticket.

"It's a ticket for the Shinkansen, the bullet train." The man informed him as if he were reading Jake's thoughts. "You're expected in Kyoto tonight."

"Kyoto?" Jake asked. A flurry of questions raced through his mind. "Who sent you? And why Kyoto?"

The man's lips curved into a faint smile. "Just go. You will find out. Just make sure you're on that train. It departs in ten minutes."

Before Jake could ask anything more, the stranger merged back into the crowd and disappeared, leaving Jake standing in bewilderment. The only evidence of their encounter was the ticket clutched in Jake's hand.

He pulled out the ticket and inspected it. It was indeed a first-class ticket to Kyoto. Jake pondered the situation and the mystery deepened. Who could possibly want him in Kyoto on such short notice? Was it Akiko? She did say to meet her here.

With the words of Taka echoing in his mind about confronting things head-on, Jake decided to get on the train. Maybe this mysterious journey held the answers he was looking for. With newfound determination, Jake made his way to the Shinkansen platform ready to face whatever awaited him in Kyoto. As Jake was contemplating the meaning behind the strange request, his eyes caught a glimpse of Akiko. She looked over at Jake as she stepped onto the train. Jake smiled and made his way over to board the waiting train.

The Shinkansen, known for its punctuality, was already filling up with passengers when Jake boarded. The sleek white bullet train stood imposingly on the platform, its nose angled and streamlined for maximum speed.

Inside, the cabin was plush with comfortable seats and modern amenities. The hum of quiet conversations surrounded him. Jake navigated through the aisles and checked the ticket for his seat number. He found it - a window seat with an unobstructed view of the passing landscape.

As he settled in, he quickly scanned the faces of the nearby passengers fully expecting to see Akiko. But she was nowhere in sight. The mystery of this sudden trip to Kyoto deepened.

With a slight jolt, the train began to move, gradually picking up speed until buildings became blurs and the urban scenery of Tokyo transitioned into the lush countryside. The Shinkansen, living up to its reputation, was incredibly smooth and silent.

Jake leaned back and tried to relax. He was still reeling from the events of last night - from the intensity of the Aikido dojo to Taka's cryptic request, and now this enigmatic journey. He decided to wait for Akiko. She was on the train. He had seen her. She must have a plan.

As the journey continued, Jake's eyelids grew heavy. He was tired, but he could not sleep. Knowing Akiko was on the train, he had to wonder where she was and what her plan could be. He looked around the cabin and still saw no sign of Akiko. He looked out the window at the farmlands as they rushed by. The last hint of sunshine peeking out from behind the rugged landscape.

The gentle chugging of the Shinkansen had whisked Jake into a dreamlike state. The soft touch of an elegant hand on his arm snapped him back to reality. Squinting against the dim lighting, Jake found himself looking into the eyes of a young woman with an enigmatic smile playing on her lips.

"Sorry to disturb you," she said in nearly flawless English, her delicate voice barely above a whisper. "You are Jake, correct?" She presented him with a meticulously crafted ticket and pointed toward the end of the train. "Your friend awaits you in the private compartments. Suite C3."

Inspecting the ticket, Jake felt a blend of excitement and trepidation. The suite number was clearly marked.

"And who might this friend be?" Jake inquired, although he knew the answer.

She winked playfully and murmured, "Patience. All in due time."

With a polite nod, Jake rose and slung his backpack over one shoulder. He began navigating the plush corridors of the train's elite section, taking in the opulence that surrounded him. The private compartments stood in stark contrast to the common coach and embodied luxury and refinement.

Reaching Suite C3, Jake paused as a flurry of thoughts raced through his mind. The muffled sound of a familiar melody floated from the room. He rapped softly on the door, anticipation building.

The door glided open to unveil a serene oasis within the speeding train. Soft ambient lighting illuminated the room and large windows granted an uninterrupted view of the picturesque landscape rushing past. Nestled comfortably in the center, holding a glass of wine, was Akiko. Her eyes sparkled with a familiar feeling of home.

"Jake," she greeted, her voice soft and inviting. "Sorry it took so long."

Jake stepped inside and the door closed gently behind him, sealing them in a world of their own. Their two souls rejoiced at the realization that it was just them, finally, for the remainder of the journey to Kyoto.

The rhythmic hum of the Shinkansen against the tracks combined with the warmth of the compartment created an atmosphere of unparalleled comfort. It wasn't long before Akiko drifted into a peaceful slumber, her head gently cradled against Jake's chest. Every so often he felt the gentle rise and fall of her breathing seemed in sync with the train's motion, and it reassured him of her presence.

Outside the window, the world was a blur of shadowy silhouettes, punctuated by the occasional glow of distant towns. Lost in his thoughts, Jake found himself marveling at the turn of events. Tokyo, Akiko, the Shinkansen — it all felt surreal.

A gentle stirring beside him brought his attention back to the present. Akiko's eyelids fluttered open, revealing deep pools of hazel that immediately sought Jake's gaze. Her lips curved into a contented smile and her fingers absently traced patterns on the back of Jake's hand.

"Did you manage to sleep?" she inquired, her voice soft and husky from her short nap.

He shook his head but a small smile graced his lips. "Not a wink. But oddly enough, I've never felt better."

Akiko propped herself up on one elbow and she studied him with an intensity that made Jake's heart race. "Jake," she began, hesitating for a moment as if she were searching for the right words. "This train, tonight... I wanted to do something special. Just us. Away from everything and everyone in Tokyo."

Jake gently squeezed her hand, signaling his attentiveness. "I have to admit. I was confused. But here we are and I couldn't be happier." He chuckled in disbelief that just hours ago he was sitting in his cubicle at the office.

She nodded. Drawing a deep breath, her eyes shimmered with love and contentment. "This is just the beginning."

Wrapped in the comforting embrace of the train and each other, the two settled into a silent communion while letting the Shinkansen carry them forward into the yawning expanse of the night.

CHAPTER THIRTEEN
Kyoto Station

The shrill whistle of the Shinkansen began to fade as it disappeared from view and was replaced by the bustling hum of Kyoto Station. A sea of faces flowed in every direction, but amid the ocean of commuters, Jake and Akiko stood out.

Stepping onto the pavement, they were immediately greeted by the glinting black sheen of a sleek limousine. The driver, a neatly-dressed man with stoic features, nodded respectfully at Akiko and held the door open for them.

Inside the limousine, plush leather seating enveloped them in luxury. A delicate scent of cedarwood filled the air, and a soft glow illuminated the space. As the limo set off, Akiko and Jake snuggled closer together, the bustling world outside replaced by a bubble of serenity.

The ancient city of Kyoto unfolded around them and offered a mesmerizing blend of the old and the new. Traditional machiya houses stood shoulder to shoulder with modern boutiques, and centuries-old temples peered through the canopy of leafy trees, bearing silent witness to the passage of time.

As the limousine turned a corner, the hotel loomed into view. A stunning edifice of glass and stone, the luxury hotel was an architectural marvel that seamlessly integrated contemporary design with traditional

Japanese aesthetics. The facade shimmered and reflected the soft golden hues of the setting sun.

Exiting the limo, Jake felt a gentle tug as Akiko intertwined her fingers with his, the gesture speaking volumes of her trust and affection. Their footfalls echoed softly on the marble floors of the grand lobby. The air was filled with a subtle scent of cherry blossoms, reminiscent of early spring in Kyoto.

Dressed in immaculate uniforms and with professionalism evident, the hotel staff bowed deeply as Akiko and Jake passed by. The attention to detail, from the intricately arranged ikebana to the soft koto music playing in the background, gave the lobby an air of understated elegance.

As they approached the front desk, a well-dressed concierge greeted them with a warm smile. "Welcome to the Kyoto Elysium, Miss Kimura. We've been expecting you."

Akiko smiled graciously and her gaze shifted to Jake. "And this is Jake. Please ensure his stay is as comfortable as mine."

"Of course, Miss Kimura. Everything has been arranged as per your instructions," the concierge replied with a nod.

With everything in place, the two made their way to the elevators hand in hand. They were ready to embark on the next chapter of their unfolding story in the historic heart of Japan.

The elevator doors slid open with a soft chime and revealed a grand entranceway. The scent of fresh flowers, a mix of elegant lilies and fragrant roses, permeated the air. Immediately, they were met with a panoramic view of Kyoto's skyline which was dominated by distant temple rooftops and the soft swells of nearby hills illuminated by a mesmerizing full moon.

As Akiko took a step forward her heels clicked on the pristine marble floors. She led Jake into the living area, where opulent furnishings in a blend of Western and traditional Japanese styles adorned the room. Large sliding glass doors led to a balcony that promised the serenity of a private garden in the sky.

"I had this suite reserved for us," Akiko said, a hint of playfulness in her voice. "As you can see, it's a two-bedroom suite. You know, so you can have your privacy."

Jake chuckled, playfully nudging her. "Oh wow thank you, I was getting nervous."

Walking around, Akiko opened the door to one of the bedrooms. It was magnificent and featured a large Western-style bed with lavish linens and an adjoining bathroom that boasted a deep soaking tub with a view. The room was accentuated with Japanese touches—tatami mats, delicate shoji screens, and a traditional tea ceremony set neatly displayed on a low table.

Jake peeked into the adjacent bedroom, which mirrored the first in opulence but had its own unique touches—a beautiful Japanese ink painting adorned the wall, and an intricately carved wooden chest sat at the foot of the bed.

The suite felt like a sanctuary, a place removed from the bustle of the world outside, where time seemed to stand still.

Akiko moved closer and her voice dropped to a whisper. "I wanted this to be special for us, Jake. A place where we could talk and get to know each other more away from the office. Away from everything."

He nodded, deeply moved by her gesture. "It's perfect, Akiko."

For a moment, they simply stood there drinking in the serenity and the promise of what the night might bring.

Jake looked around the opulent suite and admired the attention to detail and the ambiance it created. But practicality soon intruded upon his thoughts. "Akiko," he began, with a slight chuckle. "It's a beautiful suite, but we don't have any luggage or change of clothes. I mean, we're in Kyoto. Let me take us shopping."

She tilted her head, a mischievous grin forming on her lips. "Go check the closets, Jake."

Raising an eyebrow, Jake did as she suggested. He opened the sliding wooden door of one of the closets in his designated bedroom, and to his surprise found that it was filled with impeccably tailored suits, casual wear, dress shoes, and even a set of traditional Japanese yukata. It was as if a personal stylist had handpicked a wardrobe just for him.

Across the room, Akiko opened her closet to reveal a stunning array of dresses, blouses, skirts, and traditional Japanese kimonos in vibrant colors and intricate patterns. There were even matching sets of shoes and handbags for each outfit.

Jake turned to her with a playful frown on his face. "Did you…?"

Akiko's laugh was a light, bubbly sound that was infectious. "No, Jake! I didn't. The hotel offers this special service for certain guests. They can pre-arrange a personalized shopping spree based on sizes and style preferences. I just gave them our sizes and a brief about our styles. Voila! We have a wardrobe for the weekend. They even ship this back to Tokyo for us when the weekend concludes."

He shook his head in amazement as he admired a particularly sharp-looking blazer. "This is… incredible. I've never seen anything like this before."

Akiko approached and began tugging lightly at the lapel of the blazer he was holding. "Well, now we have no excuses. We can freshen up, dress up, and maybe head out for a traditional Kyoto dinner. Or we can order in and just relax. What do you think?"

Jake smiled, placed the blazer back in the closet, and turned to face Akiko. "Honestly, a quiet dinner here with you sounds perfect."

She smiled back, a warmth in her eyes. "Then, it's a date."

The evening sky over Kyoto was as black as ink, and the distant stars were starting to make their appearance. The soft glow of traditional paper lanterns from the streets below added to the magical ambiance. Akiko and Jake sat at an elegantly set table on the spacious balcony of their suite, which provided a panoramic view of the historical city.

A gentle breeze carried the distant sounds of a shamisen playing somewhere in the distance. Its melancholic notes complemented the serene setting.

They were served a traditional kaiseki meal – a multi-course Japanese dinner that reflected the seasons. Every dish was a work of art that was intricately arranged to showcase the ingredients' natural colors and flavors.

As they enjoyed the sashimi course, Jake commented, "This is possibly the best meal I've ever had. Every dish feels like a journey."

Akiko nodded and took a sip of her sake. "Kaiseki is about more than just taste. It's about experiencing the transient beauty of nature through food. Every ingredient and every flavor has its moment in the season, and the chef captures that moment for us."

They continued through the courses, from grilled dishes to steamed ones, and from rice dishes to delicate desserts. Each dish sparked a conversation – about their travels, experiences, or memories associated with a particular flavor.

Jake recalled his first experience with wasabi. "I remember thinking it was some kind of avocado paste and took a huge mouthful. My sinuses remembered that for days!"

Akiko laughed heartily and shared her own stories, like her childhood memories associated with the taste of pickled vegetables or her first experience eating fugu, the infamous blowfish.

As the meal concluded with matcha and traditional sweets, Jake leaned back feeling content. "This evening... I wish it could last forever."

Akiko's eyes shone with emotion. "It can last forever Jake. It really can."

They sat there for a while soaking in the ambiance with the city lights twinkling below and the universe above. The barriers between them seemed to melt away and were replaced by a bond that felt stronger than ever. They were now fully in love.

CHAPTER FOURTEEN
Lost and Found

The sun was shining brightly as Jake and Akiko approached the majestic Honno-Ji temple. It stood tall and proud, having borne witness to centuries of Japan's storied history. The intricate woodwork and vibrant colors of the temple gleamed under the sun, and the smell of incense wafted gently from inside, signaling a promise of calm and serenity.

Aware of the importance of this place and the story it held, Akiko started to share its tale with Jake. "This temple has seen many events, but it's most famous for one particular incident – the death of Oda Nobunaga, a daimyo who wanted to unify Japan."

Jake listened intently as he took in every detail. "Unify Japan? Wasn't Japan always one country?"

Akiko smiled gently. "Not quite. During the Sengoku period, Japan was divided among various daimyo, or feudal lords, who were constantly at war with each other. Nobunaga was the first who dreamt of a united Japan and came close to achieving it. He was ambitious and used both military and strategic prowess to gain control over most of the central region."

Walking side by side, they made their way into the temple. The peaceful atmosphere inside seemed to be in stark contrast to the violent history it was tied to.

"But his ambition was also his downfall," Akiko continued. "In 1582, while he was staying at Honno-Ji, one of his most trusted generals, Akechi Mitsuhide, turned against him. It's said that Mitsuhide's betrayal was driven by personal reasons – perhaps a grudge or a desire for power."

Jake pondered for a moment. "So, what happened?"

"Surrounded and outnumbered, Nobunaga knew he couldn't escape. So, he chose to commit seppuku, a form of ritual suicide. His death marked the end of his ambition, but it paved the way for others to complete the unification of Japan."

They stood silently for a moment as they both paid their respects. The shadows of the past seemed to linger in the air, reminding them of the complex tapestry of human emotions – ambition, betrayal, honor, and sacrifice.

As they exited the temple, Jake commented, "It's incredible how much history there is in every corner of this country. And yet, everything fits together like pieces of a puzzle."

Akiko nodded and her eyes were thoughtful. "It's true. Japan's history is a mosaic of events, and every piece tells a story. And just like Nobunaga tried to fit the pieces together, every one of us, in our own lives, tries to find where we fit in."

Jake considered her words, thinking about his journey – from Los Angeles to Tokyo, from feeling out of place to finding a sense of belonging. "I guess I'm still trying to find my place in this puzzle," he mused.

Akiko squeezed his hand reassuringly. "Jake, you have found your place. You were the missing piece to my puzzle. And I was the missing piece to yours."

Jake chuckled and shot her a playful look. "You're not going to kill me, are you?"

She teased, "Only if you eat the last piece of Sashimi." She playfully punched his arm before continuing, "I come from Samurai lineage, you know. So be careful."

Jake is impressed.

She continued, "Don't worry, I won't kill you. Unless you leave me… but then I would probably just kill myself. But don't steal my sashimi." She grinned and Jake smiled. He had no idea how serious she may actually be.

The soft glow of traditional lanterns illuminated the cobblestone streets of Gion as Jake and Akiko strolled hand in hand. The district's historical significance was palpable in the evening air. With the modern world seemingly miles away, the two were transported back in time by their surroundings.

"Gion is often associated with geisha," Akiko began, her voice soft and nostalgic. "It's one of the last places in Japan where you can still see geiko and maiko walking in their traditional kimonos, their white make-up standing out against the darkening sky."

Jake watched as Akiko's eyes danced with the memories of tales from her childhood. "They were the ultimate entertainers of their time," she continued. "Geisha were trained in various arts – singing, dancing, playing the shamisen – and they would perform at exclusive gatherings and tea houses. They were the life of the party and were revered for their grace and skill."

Looking around, Jake could almost hear the distant strains of the shamisen, the laughter of the patrons, and the clinking of sake cups. "And the samurai?" he asked, his curiosity piqued.

Akiko chuckled. "Ah, the samurai! Warriors of honor and discipline. In the Edo period, when peace prevailed, samurai were no longer just warriors; they became bureaucrats, educators, and even artists. But their code, the Bushido, remained intact. It stressed loyalty, self-discipline, and honor unto death."

She paused and looked down a narrow alley. "In these very streets, samurai would sometimes clash, dueling for honor or to settle personal vendettas. The results could be fatal with a single strike determining one's fate."

Jake looked around with newfound respect. The silent streets held echoes of the past, of lives lived with passion and purpose, of love and betrayal, and of honor above all.

"I never realized how much history is hidden in these streets," Jake admitted. "But it's not just the history, is it? It's the spirit of the people, their values, their stories. It's what makes this place alive even today."

Akiko nodded. Her face was illuminated by the soft glow of a nearby lantern. "Exactly. The past shapes us, but it's how we choose to remember and honor it that truly defines who we are."

Jake stopped. His look suddenly turned deadly serious. "I would die for you, Akiko."

She returned his stare with equal intensity. "I believe you already have."

Jake does not know what to say. Akiko continued, "In a past life. I believe you already did that for me."

Suddenly, some children pop around a corner, laughing and playing and it cut the palpable tension of the moment. Jake and Akiko looked at the kids and smiled.

They continued their walk in companionable silence, each lost in their thoughts as the stories of the past weaved a tapestry of understanding and connection between them.

The elegant suite enveloped Jake and Akiko in a cocoon of luxury.

The distant hum of Kyoto's nightlife was barely audible through the glass doors leading to the balcony. The two of them lay side by side on the vast, comfortable bed, draped in plush hotel bathrobes. The room was dimly lit and the glow from the city outside and the soft light from the television provided the only illumination.

On the screen, a classic Japanese movie played — black and white imagery of samurai and ancient landscapes. Neither of them truly followed the storyline; instead, they found comfort in the ambiance it created.

Akiko snuggled closer to Jake, her head resting on his shoulder. "Did you ever imagine watching old Japanese films in a penthouse suite in Kyoto when you first moved to Japan?" she asked with a playful tone.

Jake chuckled softly and wrapped an arm around her. "Honestly, no. My life has taken so many unexpected turns since I got here. But right now, everything feels just right."

Akiko tilted her head up to look at him, her eyes reflecting genuine curiosity. "Do you ever think about going back to LA? Starting over there?"

Jake sighed as the weight of the question sank in. "I used to. But there's something about Japan, about its culture and history... and you... that keeps me here. LA is where I grew up, but Tokyo, and even Kyoto now, feel like home."

Akiko smiled and a contented look appeared in her eyes. "You're Japanese, Jake. You always have been. I am glad you finally realized it. Welcome home." Jake smiled and Akiko kissed him on the cheek.

As they continued watching the film, the silence was filled with the gentle rhythm of their breathing and the unspoken bond they shared. The movie's dialogues, the ambiance of the suite, and the closeness they felt — everything melded together to create a serene bubble away from the outside world.

As the night deepened, Akiko's eyelids began to flutter. The events of the day were catching up with her. Jake felt her breathing even out as she drifted to sleep against him. He pressed a gentle kiss to her forehead and switched off the TV.

Lying there, with Akiko nestled close, Jake pondered the course his life had taken. From LA to Tokyo and now Kyoto, each city taught him something valuable. As he slowly drifted off to sleep, one thing was certain — he was exactly where he was meant to be.

CHAPTER FIFTEEN

Deja Voodoo

The first sensation that reached Jake as he slowly stirred from sleep was the peculiar absence of Akiko's presence beside him. The soft sheets of the bed felt colder on one side. Blinking away the last remnants of slumber, he propped himself up on one elbow and took in the vast, luxurious room that was still faintly lit with the early morning light.

A soft rustling noise drew his attention to the desk where a folded piece of paper sat beside a Shinkansen ticket. Curiosity piqued, Jake swung his legs over the side of the bed and approached the desk. The paper was adorned with Akiko's elegant handwriting. Unfolding it, he began to read:

"Jake,

I'm truly sorry for the abruptness, but I had to return to Tokyo. I didn't want to wake you. However, I've made a list of places that I strongly suggest you visit today. These are locations that carry the weight of our nation's history both its honor and its brutality. It's essential to understand these stories to truly feel the spirit of Japan and the connection we share.

1. Kiyomizu-dera: An ancient temple with a breathtaking

view of Kyoto. This place has withstood the test of time and carries stories of hope and endurance.

2. Nijo Castle: A monument to the shogunate era, complete with nightingale floors that chirp to announce intruders. You'll be taken back to the times of the samurai.

3. Sanjusangendo: A hall of a thousand Buddhas. It's a testament to our religious dedication and the craftsmanship of our ancestors.

4. Fushimi Inari Taisha: Walk through the thousands of red torii gates. Each one tells a story of dedication and devotion.

5. The Philosopher's Walk: A peaceful path along a canal. Reflect on everything you've seen and felt.

Please visit these places and open your soul to them. I'll be waiting for your stories when we reunite. Understand these places and you will understand my soul... Our souls...

With love,
Akiko"

Jake took a moment to absorb the words, then looked at the Shinkansen ticket. It was for a late evening train back to Tokyo. A whole day stretched before him and he planned to fill it with exploration and discovery.

Slipping into the clothes that had been so thoughtfully provided, Jake felt a surge of determination. He may not have Akiko by his side today, but he would honor her wishes and immerse himself fully in the depths of Japan's history.

With the list in hand, he left the suite eager to embark on a journey through time and tradition. And with each step, he could feel the weight and the legacy of the nation enveloping him and painting a vivid picture of Japan's soul.

NIJO CASTLE

The vast courtyard of Nijo Castle stretched before Jake. It was a canvas of meticulously raked pebbles and stately pine trees. Despite the few tourists milling around, there was an overpowering sense of quiet reverence, and it was as if the air itself was heavy with whispers of long-forgotten tales.

Jake slowly meandered through the grounds, his footsteps quiet against the stone path. With every step, the massive wooden gates and the ornate carvings on the castle's facade seemed to pull him deeper into Japan's past.

The feeling was almost disorienting. Every corner, every stone, every tree seemed oddly familiar. He was sure he had never been here before, but the overwhelming sensation of déjà vu gripped him. It was as if the very ground beneath him was echoing memories of a life he had once lived.

He approached the main building, and the famous nightingale floors greeted him with their characteristic chirping. Each step felt like a harmonious song that was tying him closer to the castle's storied past. The feeling intensified as he entered the chambers with the opulent tatami mat rooms and intricately painted sliding doors. In his mind's eye, he saw samurai kneeling, their armor glinting in the dim light and their stern faces masked with determination and loyalty.

Stopping in a particularly vibrant room adorned with paintings of cherry blossoms and cranes, Jake felt an almost magnetic pull to the center of the room. He sat down, folded his legs beneath him, and closed his eyes. The surroundings seemed to fade and were replaced by a vivid tapestry of memories.

He saw himself, dressed in the elaborate garb of a high-ranking samurai engaged in a heated discussion with other lords. The room was the same, but the atmosphere was thick with tension. Swords were sheathed, but the undercurrent of danger was palpable.

Shouts. A clash of metal. Suddenly, a betrayal, a fight, a desperate struggle for honor and survival. Then, as quickly as it came, the vision dissipated, leaving Jake gasping and disoriented.

Shaken, he slowly stood up, his heart racing. The memories, or whatever they were, felt too real, too visceral to be mere imagination. The weight of centuries pressed down on him, making the air thick and difficult to breathe.

Clutching Akiko's list tightly in his hand, Jake made his way out of the castle while feeling a profound connection to the land and its history. He knew he had more places to visit and more tales to uncover. But Nijo Castle had already given him an experience he would never forget.

As he exited the main gate, he couldn't help but glance back one more time, half-expecting to see a ghostly samurai nodding in acknowledgment. But all he saw was the majestic castle, standing timeless and proud, guarding its secrets for another day.

FUSHIMI INARI TAISHA

The serene pathway of Fushimi Inari Taisha was bathed in a warm golden light, the sun filtering through the dense foliage overhead. The vermilion torii gates loomed large and impressive and formed a never-ending tunnel that led Jake up the mountain. Each gate was a dedication, a prayer, and a wish – the spiritual energy was almost palpable.

As he tread carefully on the stone path, the déjà vu returned. It wasn't just the feeling of having been here, but an intense sense of belonging. It was as if this mountain and its gates held fragments of his soul.

Jake couldn't shake the feeling that each step he took was retracing steps he'd taken a long time ago. The sounds of chirping birds and distant murmurs of other visitors faded and were replaced by a haunting silence.

Upon reaching a particularly dense stretch of torii gates, a sudden gust of wind stirred the trees, and the gates seemed to shimmer and shift. Jake blinked, and the scenery altered. Instead of polished, well-maintained gates, he saw older, weathered ones, some moss-covered, others slightly askew. The air smelled different – fresher, untouched by modern pollutants. The path beneath him was not the well-trodden stone of today but a rugged, natural trail.

He was no longer a man from the 21st century, but a figure from Japan's distant past. The attire he wore felt heavier, more traditional, and at his side was a blade – a symbol of his rank and stature. On his kimono, he instantly recognized the crest of the once-great Tokugawa clan.

But more than the scenery or his attire, it was the feelings that overwhelmed Jake. A profound love, a longing, and a sense of duty. He felt ties that were strong and undeniable — to this land and to a woman whose face he could not quite recall, yet whose essence felt uncannily like... Akiko.

Reaching the mountain's peak, Jake looked out over an unspoiled Kyoto. A city not yet touched by the hands of time, technology, or tourism. A city of temples, traditional homes, and simple life. His heart swelled with emotions and feelings of pride, love, and a hint of sorrow.

A gentle touch on his shoulder snapped Jake back to the present. He turned to see a fellow tourist who was asking if he was okay. Jake nodded and took a moment to catch his breath. His heart was still racing from the intensity of the vision.

He couldn't explain it, nor did he fully understand it. But one thing was clear: Jake had lived another life here, one intertwined with Japan's rich tapestry of history and with Akiko.

Making his way back down the mountain, Jake was filled with a newfound appreciation and reverence for the land and its people. The gates, the mountain, and the city weren't just places to visit; they were keys to unlocking memories of a nearly forgotten past life. His mind raced. He needed to get back to Tokyo. Back to the woman he has loved for all of eternity. Back to Akiko.

CHAPTER SIXTEEN

Journey of Reflections

The sleek Shinkansen bullet train slid out of Kyoto Station with its characteristic elegance and hum. Inside, the rows of neatly aligned seats accommodated passengers who were each absorbed in their own world. Jake was no exception.

Positioned by the window, his gaze was unwavering, but his thoughts were far from the passing landscapes. The juxtaposition of the modern marvel that was the Shinkansen, with the age-old traditions and mysteries he'd just delved into, was not lost on him.

Each fleeting scene outside the window seemed to invoke a memory or emotion from the past few days. A streak of vermilion reminded him of the torii gates at Fushimi Inari Taisha, a patch of green evoked the tranquil gardens of Nijo Castle, and a silhouette of a mountain in the distance brought back the overwhelming emotions he'd felt at the peak.

Jake found himself pondering the ethereal connection he felt to this land. How could a man from Los Angeles feel such a deep resonance with a country that was oceans away? The visions he'd experienced, that he'd inexplicably pulled from a past he couldn't recall but felt deeply connected to, all felt so real and yet so surreal.

He remembered Akiko's touch, her voice as she recounted tales of historic Japan, and the warmth of her hand holding his. Their connection was undeniable. Was it just a product of this trip? Or was it a continuation of a bond that had transcended lifetimes?

Lost in thought, Jake barely noticed the hours passing by. Before he knew it, the train was gliding into the sprawling metropolis of Tokyo. As buildings replaced fields and the hum of the city grew louder, Jake felt an odd sense of grounding. The past days had been a whirlwind of emotion, and the familiar surroundings of Tokyo seemed like a welcome anchor to the present.

Stepping out of the train, the rush of the city enveloped him. But beneath the surface hustle, Jake carried with him the memories, feelings, and questions from Kyoto. He knew that his journey was far from over. The pieces of the puzzle were starting to come together, and Jake was eager to discover where they'd lead next.

As Jake navigated the familiar streets of his Tokyo neighborhood, each step felt both routine and renewed after his sojourn in Kyoto. The soft lighting from the street lamps created a tranquil ambiance, which, when coupled with his tiredness, made the walk back home seem almost dreamlike.

Upon reaching his apartment, he was greeted by the subtle sound of wind chimes gently swaying from his balcony. Jake paused momentarily to appreciate their melodic resonance before fumbling for his keys.

Opening the door, the first thing he saw was an envelope placed carefully on his dining table. The handwriting was unmistakably Akiko's. A soft smile tugged at his lips. He didn't even need to open it to feel its warmth. But when he did, her words swept over him like a comforting blanket.

"My Loving Jake,

Though the distance between Kyoto and Tokyo is mere hours, being away from you feels like ages. I hope our time in Kyoto brought as much wonder and reflection to you as it did for me. There's so much more I want to share and so many more memories to create.

I know you're probably exhausted after today. Sleep well, and let your dreams be filled with the magic of the Torii gates and the echoes of ancient tales. And remember, even when not beside you, I'm always with you. Always.

Yours into eternity,
Akiko."

Jake felt a powerful sense of longing for Akiko and his heart was heavy with the weight of emotions that only deep connections can bring. The apartment suddenly felt cavernous and empty without her presence. But the letter was a salve and a reminder that they were still connected despite the physical distance. Missing her was an exquisite mix of pain and pleasure.

Leaving the lights dim, Jake made his way to his bedroom. The pull of sleep grew with each passing second. He changed into comfortable attire and slipped into bed clutching Akiko's letter close to his heart.

The events of the day, coupled with the myriad emotions, had left him spent. Within minutes, Jake was fast asleep and drifting into a world where history, present, and dreams were interwoven seamlessly.

Amidst the foggy haze of dreamscape, the bustling streets of Edo-era Japan came alive. The wooden structures, woven lanterns, and the hushed murmurs of locals painted a vibrant backdrop to Jake's dream.

The normally serene environment was interrupted by a sudden altercation. Taka, dressed in the elegant garb of a Yakuza from that time, stood firm as four menacing bandits circled him. Each held a gleaming katana. Their blades shimmered ominously in the dappled light. Taka's usually calm demeanor displayed a rare mix of determination and anxiety, yet he stood his ground.

Observing this confrontation, Jake felt a rush of adrenaline. Instinctively, he stepped forward and began calling out to the bandits. "Enough of this! Stand down, now!" The authority in his voice was unmistakable. Dressed in the ornate armor of a Tokugawa Samurai with a family crest prominently displayed, Jake was an imposing figure.

The bandits halted in their tracks, instantly recognizing the emblem and the authority it represented. The leader, a man with a scar running down his cheek, took a cautious step back and lowered his weapon. "Apologies, Lord Samurai," he said with a nod, a sign of deference to Jake's status.

Taka, although relieved, still looked tense. As the bandits dispersed, Taka stepped forward and offered a deep bow to Jake. "You have my eternal gratitude, sir. It seems our destinies are intertwined." He then looked into Jake's eyes, and there was a powerful intensity behind his gaze. "In this life or any other, I vow to be by your side protecting you from any harm."

The moment was interrupted by the distant sound of temple bells. Their echo grew louder and more urgent. As the fog thickened, the figures of Taka, the bandits, and the Edo scenery began to fade, leaving Jake alonc in thc mist with the weight of Taka's promise heavy on his heart.

Suddenly, he was jolted awake.

Jake sat upright in his bed and took a moment to process the vivid dream. He could still feel the intensity of Taka's vow and hear the sincerity in his voice. Glancing at the clock, he realized it was still early. But instead of returning to sleep, he felt a need to connect with Taka and perhaps share the strange yet deeply profound dream.

He grabbed his phone from the bedside table and began dialing Taka's number while hoping that his friend was awake. Ex or not, Taka was a Yakuza. He would be awake. The night is his domain.

The phone rang several times before it was answered. Jake immediately felt that something was off when an unfamiliar voice responded.

"Who's this?" The voice was gruff and cold.

"It's Jake. I'm a friend of Taka's. Why are you answering his phone?"

There was a pause and the tension was palpable even through the distance of the call. "Taka's gone," the voice said, the words heavy and clipped.

"Gone? Gone where?" Jake's voice cracked with a mix of confusion and concern.

"That's not your concern," the voice replied curtly, leaving no room for argument. "Just... forget you called."

Before Jake could press for more information, the line went dead. The abrupt end to the call left him with an icy pit in his stomach. The weight of the dream, combined with the mysterious phone call, amplified his worries tenfold.

Jake tried calling back several times, but each attempt was met with a voicemail message. He considered heading to Taka's place, but the exhaustion of the day coupled with the mental fatigue from the strange events held him back. As much as he wanted answers, the need for rest overpowered him.

Crawling back into bed, Jake's mind raced with numerous questions and concerns about Taka's whereabouts and well-being. Every possible scenario played out in his head, from Taka being in some kind of trouble to the possibility that the dream had some real-world implications.

His mind whirred with possibilities, but sleep eventually reclaimed him and offered a reprieve from the worries of the waking world.

Morning would bring a new urgency to find Taka and uncover the truth behind the mysterious phone call. But for now, the city of Tokyo continued its nocturnal dance, oblivious to the personal mysteries unfolding within its vast expanse.

CHAPTER SEVENTEEN

Revelations

The atmosphere at Tokyo Gaming was its usual bustling self. Jake tried to drown himself in his work, but every click of the mouse or ping from an incoming email only reminded him of the mysterious call from the night before. By lunchtime, the concern for Taka was like a storm cloud that was dark and looming over his thoughts.

In a bid for answers, Jake decided to visit the bar where he had last seen Taka. Stepping in, he immediately noticed the dim lighting, the heavy scent of aged wood and alcohol, and the faint hum of hushed conversations. It was mid-day and only a few locals sat at the tables drinking and passing time. The bartender, a stocky man covered in tattoos peeking out from under his sleeves, was meticulously wiping a glass. He looked every bit the stereotype of an ex-Yakuza, from the scars on his knuckles to the piercing gaze that seemed to have seen more than most could handle.

Mustering courage, Jake approached the bar. "I'm looking for Taka. Have you seen him?"

The bartender's eyes locked onto Jake's for a heartbeat that felt like an eternity. He then simply asked, "You're Jake?"

Jake nodded and was slightly taken aback that the bartender knew his name. Without a word, the bartender reached under the bar and handed Jake a sealed envelope. It was thin and felt slightly heavier than just paper. Jake turned it over to see his name written in Taka's neat handwriting.

Opening the note, Jake's heart raced as he read:

"Jake,

If you're reading this, it means I'm dead. But know this. You were my only true friend in this city. A beacon in the darkness. Check inside the bag at your place. I've left something for you. It's a token of my appreciation for your unwavering friendship.

Taka."

Jake's emotions swirled between confusion, concern, and surprise. As he pocketed the note, he looked up to thank the bartender but was met with a nod of acknowledgment and respect from the steely-eyed man. The bartender added, "Taka respected you. And Taka didn't respect many people."

Jake is stunned, "Taka... is dead?" The bartender nodded solemnly. Jake continued, "How? What happened?" The bartender shook his head with a steely glare. Jake was too stunned to speak or to even move. He fought back his emotions with everything he had.

The weight of the situation settled heavily on Jake's shoulders. What had happened to Taka? And what had he left behind?

Jake returned to his apartment with a singular focus. Unlocking the door, he quickly got under his bed and found the small, nondescript bag. With a mixture of sadness and trepidation, he opened it.

Inside was an intricately carved wooden box. Opening the box revealed an ornate dagger with a beautifully crafted handle and a note:

"Jake, this dagger is my honor. My soul. I will be by your side, even if you cannot see me."

Taka."

As Jake examined the dagger, realization dawned. This was no ordinary knife; it was a tanto, a traditional Japanese dagger that had significant cultural and historical value. It was old. Very old. Jake's mind raced as he tried to piece together the events and their implications.

Jake's return to the office was anything but normal. The room was a blur of screens, keyboards, and the usual chatter of colleagues discussing their tasks. Yet, amidst the ordinary, Jake felt like an alien in his world.

He tried to immerse himself in the rows and columns of data on his computer screen, but the numbers seemed to dance and blur. Every tap of the keyboard echoed Taka's absence. The weight of the tanto that was carefully tucked into his bag served as a constant reminder of the mysterious and perhaps perilous world he had unknowingly become a part of.

Glancing across the sea of desks, he caught a glimpse of the staircase that led to the upper floor where Akiko's office was located. He wondered if she was there, ensconced behind her desk, unaware of the turmoil below. Or perhaps she too was caught up in this mysterious web? The thought of her being in any danger made his heart race.

Jake wanted nothing more than to rush upstairs, confide in Akiko, and share the weight of the revelations with someone who understood. But he hesitated. Their secret relationship was still in its fragile stages, and the Tokyo Gaming environment was rife with rumors and office politics. One wrong move and the world they had built together could come crashing down.

He took a deep breath and tried to steady himself. In his drawer, he found a picture of a serene Japanese garden. It was a memento from one of his trips. Focusing on the calm pond and the perfectly placed stones, he tried to find clarity.

A message notification snapped him out of his reverie. It was from Osamu.

"Jake, you okay? Let's grab a drink if you want to talk."

Jake responded with a simple thumbs-up emoji. Maybe talking to Osamu would help him find some answers or at least provide a reprieve from the storm of thoughts. As he leaned back in his chair, his eyes again drifted to the staircase leading to Akiko's office, seeking comfort in the knowledge that she was close, even if out of reach for now.

Jake's colleague, Yumi, had always been diligent with her work, but there was something different in her demeanor today. A subtle tension. An urgency. The way her fingers tapped lightly on the stack of papers, conveyed her impatience. Her eyes darted from Jake to the other side of the office and back to Jake again.

"These are the new marketing materials, Jake," she said, brushing a strand of hair behind her ear. "Masuda-san was quite specific. He wants your feedback, if possible, by tomorrow morning. Please share any thoughts you have."

Jake's initial thought was to tell Yumi that now wasn't the best time. But seeing her obvious anxiety, and the importance Masuda seemed to have placed on this task, he nodded. "Of course, Yumi. I'll have a look."

Yumi visibly relaxed and her shoulders dropped a fraction. "Thank you," she said and gave him a small smile before hurrying back to her department.

Jake glanced at the stack of papers. Marketing strategies, projections, target audiences — it was a comprehensive plan. He flipped through the pages and skimmed the headlines. As he thumbed through, a photograph fell out. It was a beautiful shot of Kyoto with its golden temples contrasting sharply with the deep hues of autumn. And there, in the bottom right corner, was a small heart drawn with an ink pen, and inside it, the initials "A.K."

Jake's heart raced. This was Akiko's way of sending him a message. A way of expressing her feelings without openly revealing them to the world of the office. A secret "I love you" hidden amidst corporate plans.

He couldn't help but smile as he felt the weight of his worries lighten just a bit. It was amazing how a small gesture could change one's perspective.

Taking a deep breath, Jake packed the marketing plans, along with the photo, into his drawer and locked it. Regardless of what lay ahead, he was now certain of one thing: he wasn't alone.

CHAPTER EIGHTEEN

Two Become One

The city lights of Tokyo cast an electric glow on everything, painting the world in a palette of blues, pinks, and yellows. The towering skyscrapers with their geometric designs loomed over Jake as he left the Tokyo Gaming offices. The buzz of conversations from salarymen and young couples filled the air.

As Jake meandered through the streets, it was hard not to be caught up in the sights and sounds of couples in love. Young lovebirds laughing together as they shared takoyaki from a street vendor, an older couple holding hands as they strolled along the pavement, and a pair sitting closely on a bench whispering sweet nothings to each other.

Each interaction was a sharp reminder of what he and Akiko were missing out on — the freedom to be openly together without the looming shadow of office politics and workplace whispers.

He recalled their stolen moments, their secret meetups, and the careful avoidance of public places where they might be recognized. He remembered the joy of being with her and the pain of always having to part so they could return to their separate worlds. But he also remembered the thrill, the anticipation, and the passion that came from being in a secret relationship.

Yet, more than anything, he wanted to feel the normalcy that the couples around him took for granted. To hold Akiko's hand while they strolled down the streets of Shinjuku or to share an intimate dinner in a Roppongi restaurant without constantly watching over their shoulder.

Lost in his thoughts, Jake found himself standing outside his apartment building staring up at his window. The soft glow of the light from inside beckoned him. But, just as he was about to enter the building, a hand gently touched his shoulder.

He turned around, expecting to see a friend or perhaps a neighbor only to find that it was Akiko. Her face glowed softly in the city lights and her eyes brimmed with emotion.

"Hi," she whispered. The weight of the word carried more meaning than a simple greeting.

"Hi," Jake replied. His voice was laced with surprise at her appearance.

Akiko stepped closer, her hand still on Jake's shoulder. "I know it's complicated," she began, her voice wavering. "But, I don't want to hide anymore. We should talk."

Jake looked deep into her eyes, seeing his reflections of love and yearning mirrored back. "Neither do I. I was just looking at all of the couples on the street holding hands."

She raised her hand for Jake to stop talking. A slightly tormented look filled her eyes. "Can we go upstairs and talk?"

Jake sensed a seriousness, so he nodded yes. The familiar hum of Jake's apartment enveloped them both, but in the presence of one another, even familiar surroundings felt different. The soft yellow light from the corner lamp created a warm, intimate ambiance.

As Akiko sat perched on the edge of Jake's bed, her fingers lightly played with a tassel on one of the cushions. Respecting the traditional Japanese custom of not wearing shoes indoors, Jake was seated cross-legged on the tatami mats on the floor. There was a palpable tension in the room and a mixture of excitement and trepidation as they found themselves navigating new territory.

Jake broke the silence first. "This feels so different, having you here. In a good way."

Akiko smiled a gentle, sweet smile. "It does. It's like our worlds are merging. Like those two rivers we saw in Kyoto, remember? Different colors, but they flow together."

Jake nodded. "The Kamo River and the Takano River. They blend seamlessly and create something beautiful."

The analogy wasn't lost on either of them. Just like the rivers, Jake and Akiko were two distinct individuals who were gradually coming together to form a harmonious union.

"Jake," Akiko began, her voice soft and thoughtful. "I've been doing a lot of thinking about us and the risks and challenges of our relationship."

Jake leaned forward and rested his elbows on his knees. "I have been too, Akiko. I want to be with you, openly. I don't want to keep sneaking around, worrying about who might see us."

Akiko shifted and drew her legs up beneath her. "I agree. And the more I think about it, the more I realize that love shouldn't be hidden. I want the whole world to know I love you."

Jake's heart swelled with emotion. "I can leave the company. I can get another job no problem. I will figure it out."

Akiko took a deep breath. "I don't think that will be needed."

Jake nodded in agreement. "I don't want to, but I will if it means we don't have to hide...?"

Akiko reached out and intertwined her fingers with Jake's. "You're very sweet. I love you," she echoed.

He nodded. "I love you too. I really do."

The weight of their shared decision seemed to lighten the atmosphere. They leaned closer, their foreheads touching, and eyes closed as they cherished the bond they shared. Jake continued, "And we have a lot to talk about... After you left Kyoto—"

Akiko cut him off. "Dinner?"

He nodded. "I can run down and bring something up? Sushi sound good?"

Akiko stood up and held out her outstretched hand to Jake. "Let's go out. Like a regular couple?" Her eyes glimmered. "And we can talk about Kyoto."

Jake nodded yes and stood up. "Here, in Tokyo? Is that... Okay?"

She nodded. "It will be fine."

CHAPTER NINETEEN

Memories Etched in Time

Inside the elegant confines of the restaurant, the soft glow of ambient lighting reflected off the crystal glasses and silverware and cast a romantic hue over the entire dining area. It was a place that spoke of history and luxury and had a quiet grandeur that hinted at the many conversations and confessions that had been shared over the years. The faint tinkling of a piano filled the room and became a soft soundtrack to the murmurs and whispers of diners.

Akiko and Jake sat across from each other at a table by the window with the Tokyo skyline dazzling in the background. Their hands touched lightly over the table and their eyes locked in a meaningful gaze.

After a few moments of comfortable silence, Akiko took a deep breath. Her fingers nervously played with the delicate stem of her wine glass. "Jake," she began, her voice quivering, "there's something I've been meaning to tell you, something I should have told you before."

Jake tilted his head and offered her an encouraging smile. "You can tell me anything, Akiko. You know that."

She swallowed hard. "I've applied for a leave of absence from the company. I have a health condition that I need to address." She watched for a response. Jake was frozen and confused.

"Health condition?"

She nodded. "Yes, and I am afraid it's serious."

His heart sank, and a thousand thoughts raced through his mind, but he maintained his composure and squeezed her hand gently for reassurance. "We'll get through it, Akiko. Whatever it is. I am sure you will be fine. I will take care of you. Anything you need."

She gave him a faint smile as tears glistened in her eyes. "That's just it, Jake. I don't know how much time we have. I may be okay. But maybe not. Either way, I want every moment to be with you. Every second and every breath. I want you to move in with me."

Jake's heart raced. "Are you sure?"

She looked deeply into his eyes and determination shone through her tears. "And I want to marry you, Jake. Right away. Not for the formalities or the legalities, but for us. For the love we share. And yes, I am sure. Do you want to marry me?"

Jake was stunned but felt a deep warmth surge through him. "Akiko... I love you. I want nothing more than to be with you. There is nobody else for me. Of course, I will marry you. But...isn't that...rushed?"

She composed herself. "There's something else. I have savings and investments which amount to millions of dollars. We won't ever have to worry about money. I just want our remaining days to be full of happiness, joy, and love. I want to experience life with you. And not have to think about work."

Jake looked at her and felt overwhelmed. "Akiko, it's not the money that matters. It's you. It's us. And you will be fine. We will have so many years together. I don't care about money. I just want you."

She smiled and tears began streaming down her face. "I know, Jake. But I wanted you to know. What's mine is yours. Ours."

Jake got a flash of emotion. He cannot lose another person he is close to. Akiko noticed. "Are you okay?"

Jake nodded. He does not want to tell her about Taka. Not right now. Akiko asked, "Kyoto..?"

Jake is frozen. She studied his face for a reaction. "It feels like you already know what happened in Kyoto..." Jake adds.

Akiko nodded intently. "When I first...developed feelings for you...I went to see somebody to understand our connection...and yes, I do. I fully understand. That is why you needed to experience it."

Jake and Akiko were locked in a moment when a server approached. The server stood unnoticed for a long moment before Jake looked up. Akiko then looked up, startled.

Time had passed and the night had grown late. The bustling streets of Shinjuku, Tokyo were now quiet. A romantic feeling is in the air. Jake and Akiko stepped out of the restaurant and onto the sidewalk. Akiko had a youthful, girlish energy about her. She pulled Jake in close and kissed him.

Jake kissed her and then immediately looked around. She smiled. "It's okay. We are free. I have never felt more free in my entire life."

Jake smiled. He looked up at the restaurant façade. "I will never forget this place or this night."

They peered deeply into each other's eyes. Akiko is focused on Jake. "Walk me home?"

He replied, "Of course."

She continued, "But don't leave? Stay with me?"

Jake hesitated. "That sounds great, but maybe I should go home and get some things?"

She persisted. "I don't want to be away from you. Not even for a minute. We can get your things tomorrow?"

He nodded. "Okay, let's go..."

She grinned. " Yes, let's go home. To our home."

They both smiled as they made their way to the train station. The pain of loss and the concern around Taka's circumstances was temporarily pushed far from Jake's mind.

The polished wooden door to Akiko's apartment swung open to reveal an expanse of opulence and refined taste. The muted gold and deep blues of the decor were illuminated by the gentle lights that revealed stunning art pieces and elegant furniture. It was evident that the space was designed with thought and care. Each piece reflected a little bit of Akiko's soul.

Jake took a tentative step inside and let his gaze sweep over the sprawling living area, the minimalist kitchen, and the grand piano positioned by floor-to-ceiling windows. Beyond the windows, the Tokyo skyline sparkled and added a touch of magic to the scene.

"It's... incredible," Jake murmured, both referring to the apartment and the whirlwind of emotions that had swept them up in the past few hours.

Akiko chuckled softly and her eyes twinkled. "I'm glad you like it. I've lived here for years, but it always felt a little too big for just me. You are the first man to ever set foot in my home. And the last."

Jake wandered over to a wall adorned with a tapestry of cranes in flight, and his fingers gently traced the intricate stitching. "Everything's happened so quickly, hasn't it? Just days ago, we were sneaking glances at each other in the office, and now... and you're sure about me?"

Akiko walked over to him and wrapped her arms around his waist from behind. "Life has a funny way of accelerating when you least expect it. But I have no regrets, Jake. Not about us."

He turned to face her and cupped her face in his hands. "Neither do I. But are you sure about this? About me moving in so soon?"

She nodded and her eyes brimmed with certainty. "More than anything, I want you close. Time feels so fleeting, and I want to soak in every moment with you."

Jake pressed his forehead against hers as the reality of the situation began sinking in. "I love you, Akiko. I'm here with you through everything."

They stood there for a moment wrapped up in each other's embrace as the world outside faded away. The rapid pace of their relationship was daunting, but the strength of their connection made every step feel right.

After a while, Akiko pulled away slightly, a playful glint in her eye. "Come on, let me give you a tour. Especially to what will now be our bedroom."

Jake laughed. The weight on his heart momentarily lifted. Hand in hand, the pair wandered through the apartment. They were getting familiar with what would soon be their shared sanctuary in the heart of Tokyo.

It was 3 a.m. and the Tokyo skyline twinkled with a knowing that two hearts had rekindled a love that had burned for centuries.

Jake and Akiko lay in bed talking about their ancient connection. Akiko rested her head on Jake's bare chest. Jake said, "I mean yes, that blows my mind, but it makes total sense."

Akiko tilted her head to look up. "We have been together through many, many lifetimes. Here in Tokyo, or Edo as it was then, and also in Kyoto as you saw."

Jake nodded. "And felt."

She rested her head back in the comfortable spot on Jake's chest. Jake looked down toward her face to make eye contact. "And this life will be amazing too. We are going to have many beautiful years together. Trust me, I will take care of you. No matter what."

She grinned without looking up. "You always have."

CHAPTER TWENTY

Empty Offices

The soft light of morning filtered through the sheer curtains of Akiko's bedroom and cast a gentle glow over the room. The hum of Tokyo in the early hours was subdued and allowed the room to be bathed in tranquility.

Jake stirred and felt the warmth of Akiko beside him. He turned his head to watch her as her chest rose and fell into a rhythm of peaceful sleep. He gently brushed a stray hair from her face and marveled at the way the light caught her features.

As the alarm on his phone buzzed softly, he reached out to silence it, careful not to disturb her. Slowly extracting himself from the covers, he padded to the bathroom to begin his morning routine.

Emerging from the shower wrapped in a towel, he found Akiko sitting up, her deep-set eyes observing him with a quiet intensity.

"Good morning," he whispered, leaning down to plant a soft kiss on her forehead.

She smiled, her lips slightly parted. "Morning. You're going into the office?"

Jake nodded and began pulling on a crisp white shirt. "Yes, I've got meetings lined up. Are you coming in later?"

Akiko hesitated, her fingers twisting the edge of the bedsheet. "No,

I am seeing the doctor at ten."

Jake paused, his hands still on his tie. "Want me there?"

She tried to offer a reassuring smile, but it didn't quite reach her eyes. "It's just a follow-up. I am going over to meet with the wedding planner after."

He sat down beside her, the weight of her earlier revelation still fresh in his mind. "Do you want me to come with you?"

Akiko took his hand and intertwined their fingers. "I'll be fine. But thank you. I just... I want to handle this on my own today."

Jake pressed his lips to her knuckles. "Okay, just let me know if you need anything. And call me once it's done?"

She nodded and her eyes misted over slightly. "Of course. Now, you better head out or you'll be late."

Jake nodded, pulled on his sportscoat, and grabbed his backpack. Before heading to the door, he paused, turning to look at Akiko. "I love you," he whispered.

She smiled, her eyes softening. "I love you too."

As the door closed behind him, Akiko let out a shaky breath and gathered her strength for the day ahead.

At the Tokyo Gaming offices, the usual hum of activity seemed dulled. Jake's footsteps echoed a little louder, and the space felt a bit emptier without Akiko's presence. Her absence was like a void that reminded Jake of the challenges they faced and the uncertainties of the future. But in the midst of it all, their love remained the one constant, and it was guiding them through every twist and turn.

In the sterile environment of the doctor's office, Akiko sat on the examination table trying to mask her unease. With its white walls and clinical ambiance, the room always made her feel a bit detached as if she was floating above reality.

The doctor, a stern but kind-hearted woman named Dr. Saito, adjusted her glasses and skimmed through Akiko's medical records on her tablet.

"So you're planning a wedding? That's wonderful news, Akiko," Dr. Saito commented, looking up at her with a sincere smile.

Akiko returned the smile, though hers was slightly forced. "Yes, Jake and I... it feels right."

Dr. Saito placed the tablet down on the desk beside her. "Akiko, I understand that this is an exciting time for you, but it's essential for you to remember your condition. The treatments and medications you're on might cause some unpredicted side effects."

"I know, Doctor," Akiko responded, her fingers fidgeting in her lap.

Dr. Saito leaned forward slightly, her expression serious. "One of the potential side effects is mood swings, possibly even bouts of depression or anxiety. It's crucial to understand that these feelings, if they arise, are chemically induced and not your fault."

Akiko nodded while absorbing the information. "I've felt... a little more emotional lately. I just thought it was the stress."

"It could very well be a combination. Stress can exacerbate these side effects," Dr. Saito explained. "But it's essential to communicate with fiancee. Make him aware of what you might be going through, so he can support you."

"I don't want him to worry," Akiko whispered, her voice breaking slightly.

Dr. Saito reached out to place a comforting hand on Akiko's. "He loves you. And he should understand and be there for you. You don't have to go through this alone."

Taking a deep breath and bowing her head slightly, Akiko nodded. "Thank you, Doctor."

Dr. Saito gave her a reassuring smile. "We'll keep monitoring your condition closely. And remember, focus on the happiness and love in your life. Those can be just as powerful as any medicine."

Akiko left the clinic with a heavy heart, but also with the resolve to face her challenges head-on with Jake by her side.

Jake's fingers danced over his keyboard as he tried to concentrate on the task at hand. The gentle hum of the office's air conditioner and the soft chatter of his colleagues blended into a soothing white noise. However, despite the familiar setting, his thoughts were miles away with Akiko.

His phone buzzed, causing him to jump a little. Eagerly, he checked the message: *The appointment went well, love. Heading to the wedding planner now. Talk later. x*

Jake felt a weight lift from his chest, but a sudden urge took over him. He wanted to be there and to be part of every moment leading up to their union. He quickly saved his work, stood up from his desk, and slipped on his jacket. Making his way to the elevator, he passed his colleague. "Taking a break, Yumi. I'll be back soon."

The crisp Tokyo air greeted him as he stepped out of the office building. He spotted a small flower stand on the corner and its vibrant blooms beckoning him. Without hesitation, he picked out a bunch of Akiko's favorites: delicate white lilies interspersed with soft pink roses. The elderly vendor wrapped them neatly in brown paper, and with a nod of thanks, Jake set off in the direction of the wedding planner's office.

He felt a mix of excitement and nervousness as he approached the office. A small bell jingled as he entered the reception area and the scent of fresh flowers and scented candles filled the air. Akiko sat with her back to him and was deeply engrossed in conversation with the wedding planner. Jake gently cleared his throat to draw her attention.

She turned, her eyes widening in surprise. "Jake?"

He stepped forward, the bouquet held out in front of him. "Thought I'd surprise you."

A radiant smile spread across her face and her eyes glistened. "You always do."

The wedding planner chuckled. "Well, this just proves how perfect you two are for each other."

Jake handed her the bouquet of beautiful flowers and smiled at her. "I have to get back to the office, but just wanted to surprise you." Akiko looked deeply into Jake's eyes. She is moved beyond words.

He nodded politely at the wedding planner and then focused his eyes back on Akiko. "Call me if you need me. I love you." With that, he left the wedding planner's office and dashed out to the busy street.

The serenity of Akiko's apartment, with the soft glow of candles and the distant hum of Tokyo's urban soundscape, seemed far removed from the bustling life outside. As they sat on her plush couch, Akiko's fingers gently brushed Jake's hand.

"Jake," she murmured, lost in thought. "Do you ever wonder how Tokyo looks from a distance at night?"

He looked at her, a hint of surprise in his eyes. "The lights, the buildings… it's like a living painting."

Akiko's face lit up, her eyes full of mischief. "Then let's go see it!"

Jake chuckled. "Let's go. I know a place."

She nodded enthusiastically and began pulling him off the couch. "Show me!"

They slipped into their shoes, and hand in hand, ventured out into the Tokyo night. Jake led the way to a place he had discovered during one of his solitary evening walks—a bridge overlooking the Sumida River that provided a panoramic view of Tokyo's glittering skyline.

As they reached the middle of the bridge, they leaned against the railing, the cool metal pressing into their backs. Tokyo's skyline stretched out before them and the lights shimmered and reflected in the calm waters of the Sumida River. The Tokyo Skytree towered majestically in the distance, its spire piercing the night sky, glowing softly in a myriad of colors.

Jake turned to face Akiko and took both of her hands in his. "Akiko," he began, his voice soft but full of emotion, "from the moment we met, my life has been a whirlwind of feelings, adventures, and moments I never want to forget. Standing here, with Tokyo's lights surrounding us, I promise you this—I will love you forever. I want to remember every moment, every smile, every tear, every adventure we have together."

Akiko's eyes glistened with tears and the lights from the city danced in her irises. "Jake, you have this amazing way of making every moment special. I love you more than I ever thought possible. I just want us to enjoy whatever time..."

Jake softly put his finger to her mouth for her to stop. As he pulled her into a tender embrace, the lights of Tokyo formed a luminescent halo around them. They stood there, and the world seemed to pause, allowing them a moment of pure, undisturbed love and happiness.

CHAPTER TWENTY-ONE

Unraveling

ONE MONTH LATER

The Tokyo Gaming offices were buzzing with activity. Developers, designers, marketers, and managers all moved about, discussing projects, testing games, and sharing feedback. The hum of the office was almost hypnotic and provided a familiar backdrop to Jake's workday.

Just as Jake settled into a rhythm, editing some codes and chatting with a colleague about potential game updates, his cell phone vibrated with an incoming call. He didn't recognize the number but decided to answer it. "Hello?"

"Jake-san?" The voice on the other end was calm yet filled with concern. It was Hiroshi, the doorman from their upscale apartment complex. "You need to come home immediately. Akiko-san... she collapsed in the lobby. We've taken her up to your apartment. I am with her now, but you need to come."

Jake's heart sank, and his face went pale. "I'm on my way!" He grabbed his bag while murmuring apologies to his colleagues and dashed out of the office.

Tokyo's sprawling metropolis, which was usually a vibrant and exciting cityscape, now seemed like a maze of impediments. Every traffic light felt like an eternity and every crowded crosswalk a barrier.

Finally, Jake reached their building. His breath was ragged from the combination of panic and haste. Hiroshi met him at the entrance. His usually composed face was now drawn with worry. "She's upstairs," he whispered, guiding Jake to the elevator.

When the elevator doors opened to their floor, Jake nearly sprinted to their door to fling it open. There, on the couch, lay Akiko, pale and still, with a wet cloth on her forehead. Her breathing was shallow but steady.

"Akiko," Jake whispered, dropping to his knees beside her. Gently, he took her hand and felt its coldness seep into his skin.

Hiroshi cleared his throat gently. "I called for an ambulance, but she woke up and insisted she didn't want to go to the hospital. I didn't know what else to do, so I stayed with her until you arrived."

Jake nodded, still in shock, his eyes never leaving Akiko's face. "Thank you, Hiroshi. I'll take it from here."

After Hiroshi left, Jake carefully scooped Akiko into his arms and carried her to their bedroom. He tucked her in and brushed strands of hair from her face. He was wracked with worry and filled with questions. Why had she collapsed? What was happening?

He remembered the doctor's warnings about her health, her mood swings, and the stress of the wedding preparations. It all started to make sense. Jake decided then and there that Akiko's health was his number one priority. He would be there for her, supporting and caring for her, no matter what.

As he sat beside her, watching over her, the weight of responsibility pressed on him. But it was a weight he was more than willing to bear—for love and for Akiko.

Jake made his way to the opulent wedding planning agency situated in one of Tokyo's upscale neighborhoods. The plush, cream-colored carpets, and delicate chandeliers provided a stark contrast to the chaos he felt inside.

He was immediately met by Mizuki, their wedding planner. Her poised and professional demeanor never wavered, even when faced with the most challenging of tasks. "Jake-san," she greeted with a courteous bow. "What can I do for you today?"

"I'd like to move the wedding up," Jake began, trying to sound as composed as possible, "to next week."

Mizuki blinked, surprised. But she recovered quickly and tilted her head in thought. "That's certainly a tight timeline, but I believe we can make it happen. Akiko-san and you have chosen many of the details already. Let me see..." She pulled out a planner thick with notes and began flipping through its pages rapidly. "Yes, I think we can manage it."

Jake sighed with relief. "Thank you, Mizuki-san. It means a lot."

"Is everything alright?" she asked, looking concerned.

Jake hesitated, not wanting to divulge too much. "Akiko isn't well, and we want to make sure we have our wedding while she can still enjoy it."

Understanding dawned on Mizuki's face. "Say no more," she said gently. "We will make this happen. I'll start making calls right away. Please tell Akiko-san that I said hello, and to feel better."

"Thank you," Jake murmured. The gratitude was evident in his voice. He left the office feeling as though a small weight had lifted off his shoulders. The wedding was in capable hands, and all he had to do now was be there for Akiko.

As he made his way home, his heart swelled with a mix of emotions—love for Akiko, worry for her health, and gratitude for the people around them who were making their dream wedding a possibility against all odds.

The dim, ambient lighting of their apartment provided a soft glow as Jake and Akiko sat together on their plush white couch, hands intertwined. The silence enveloped them. It was a comfortable quiet that was punctuated only by the distant hum of Tokyo's nighttime hustle.

Jake broke the silence and kept his voice gentle but firm. "Akiko, maybe we could try a holistic approach? We could go on a pure vegetable diet and even start regular sauna treatments. I've read they can help detoxify and improve overall health."

Akiko looked at Jake and her almond eyes glistened in the soft light, hinting at the storm of emotions she felt within. She shook her head slowly. "Jake," she began, her voice soft and tender. "I appreciate your concern and your research, truly. But I want to enjoy every flavor life offers now. Every dish. Every dessert. I don't want to spend our limited days together on a stringent regimen."

Jake sighed and ran a hand through his hair, exasperation and worry evident in his features. "I want to fight this. I'm not giving up," he murmured.

Akiko moved closer and cupped his face with her soft hands. "I know," she whispered, "and I love you for it. But what I need now is to make the most of every moment we have, not in the hope of adding days to our life but life to our days."

He looked deep into her eyes and understood her desire to live with no regrets. "All right," he said, pulling her into a tight embrace. "We'll do it your way. Whatever you want."

She snuggled into his embrace and let the warmth and safety of his arms wash over her. "Just promise me," she murmured, her voice barely audible, "that we'll face whatever comes together."

"I promise," Jake whispered back before sealing his commitment with a gentle kiss on her forehead.

Chapter Twenty-Two

The Day Before the Wedding

The Tokyo Gaming office hummed with the energy of a typical workday, though for Jake, nothing about this day felt typical. Tomorrow, he would marry Akiko. The thought alone made it hard for him to concentrate on the game design document in front of him. Every sentence he read reminded him of the vows he'd soon be making. Every line drawn took the shape of Akiko's smiling face in his mind.

His phone buzzed and broke his trance. A message from Akiko lit up the screen. *"Jake, I'm downstairs. Come say hi?"*

A smile crept across Jake's face. He didn't need any more prompting. He quickly saved his work, grabbed his coat, and made his way downstairs.

As he approached the building's entrance, he spotted Akiko. She was leaning against a pillar, a playful grin on her face and an air of excitement surrounding her. The pallor and fatigue that had plagued her in recent days seemed to have lessened and was replaced by a radiant glow.

"Couldn't stay away, could you?" Jake teased as he approached.

Akiko laughed and her eyes danced with mischief. "Maybe I just wanted to make sure you weren't getting cold feet."

He took her hand, squeezing it gently. "Never. I've been counting the minutes."

She leaned in and gave him a gentle kiss. "Me too. I just... I felt good today and wanted to see you, even if it's just for a few minutes."

Jake smiled as a feeling of warmth spread through him. "I'm glad you did. It makes tomorrow seem even more real."

The two of them stood there for a few moments, lost in each other. The bustling streets of Tokyo moved around them, but they remained still as two souls about to intertwine forever.

"I should let you get back to work," Akiko said finally, regret evident in her voice. "But remember, tomorrow, you're all mine."

Jake chuckled. "I have been all yours since the moment we met. Even though you said I smelled like cigarettes."

She grinned. "I was all yours in that very moment too. No matter what I said."

Akiko looked up at Jake sweetly. "Remember, be home by 7 so we can get over to the hotel?"

Jake nodded. "About the hotel. Are we still doing the separate rooms?"

She grinned. "Yes, silly. Separate rooms."

He pulled her close. "I just want to spend every moment with you, you get that right?"

She flashed an inviting smile. "Well, if you want some one-on-one time before we go to the hotel, be home by 5?"

He nodded. "You're on. I will be home by 5."

They shared one more lingering kiss before Jake headed back inside, the weight of his responsibilities momentarily lightened by the promise of their shared future.

The clock on the wall showed 4:30 pm as Jake logged off his computer. He'd worked through lunch to make sure he could leave early and savor the quiet before the storm of activity that would be their wedding day. He was eager to return home, to see Akiko, and to share a few precious, intimate moments before the whirlwind.

Stepping out of the Tokyo Gaming offices, the autumn air was crisp, and the city was beginning to glow as the sun started its descent. Jake maneuvered through the bustling crowd, each step quickening with the anticipation of being with Akiko.

He arrived at the luxury apartment complex where they shared a home, its facade reflecting the golden hues of the evening sun. The doorman greeted him with his usual professionalism but with a hint of concern that seemed to be hiding a secret.

"Good evening, Jake-san. You just missed Akiko-san," the doorman said.

"She left already?" Jake asked, expecting her to be upstairs getting ready for their pre-wedding evening at the hotel.

The doorman's expression didn't waver, but his next words injected a note of confusion into the evening. "Oh, Akiko-san left for the hotel about an hour ago. She mentioned that she needed to prepare some final details."

Jake's brows furrowed slightly. It wasn't like Akiko to change plans without telling him, especially not today. "Did she say why she left early?"

The doorman shook his head. "No, she didn't. Just that you should come to the hotel when you are ready."

A mix of surprise and a touch of concern nudged at Jake's composure. He thanked the doorman and headed upstairs to drop off his bag and freshen up. The apartment was quiet, and the silence amplified his sense of unease. There was a note on the kitchen counter in Akiko's elegant script.

"Jake,

I needed to get a head start. I wanted to make sure everything was perfect. Meet me at the hotel. I can't wait to start our lives together.

Love, Akiko."

Jake read the note twice, then three times while looking for something in the words that might hint at why she had left early. But there was nothing—just the same love and anticipation that they both felt for the day ahead.

He took a deep breath and allowed the simple fact that Akiko was excited to wash away the remnants of his worry. He changed his clothes and grabbed the overnight bag they had packed together the night before. He was ready.

As he made his way to the hotel, he thought about the first time he saw her, the first time they laughed together, and the first time they realized this was more than a simple fling. And now, on the eve of their wedding, the journey felt both incredibly long and as fleeting as a cherry blossom in the wind.

When Jake arrived at the luxurious hotel, its lobby was bathed in the soft light of chandeliers. The concierge directed him to his suite. As he opened the door, he expected to find Akiko, her back to him, lost in the view of the city, or perhaps pouring over the seating chart one last time. But the room was empty and was a reminder that he would not be seeing her tonight. The next time he saw her, they would be trading their vows.

The view from the window was indeed breathtaking, but it couldn't hold Jake's gaze. He was missing Akiko. He felt incomplete without her.

In a suite, just one floor above where Jake stood missing her, the room was suffused with the dusky light of a setting sun. Akiko stood by the expansive window, her silhouette etched against the sprawling cityscape of Tokyo. The vibrant life of the city moved beneath her and was a stark contrast to the stillness that enveloped her.

The reflection in the glass didn't just show a woman in a luxurious hotel room; it showed her vulnerabilities, the tremble in her lip, the moisture that made her eyes glisten, and the slow tears that streamed down her cheeks.

The room around her was scattered with the beautiful trappings of their upcoming celebration. Petals and soft silk, envelopes with elegantly scripted names, and tiny boxes of favors for the guests. But all the preparations and all the careful plans seemed to weigh heavily on her.

Akiko turned away from the window while drawing in a deep, shuddering breath as she attempted to compose herself. The wedding was less than a day away, and every detail had been seen to with meticulous care. Yet, there she was, a bride-to-be, grappling with a maelstrom of emotions she could hardly articulate.

A single photograph lay on the vanity—a picture of her with Jake, their smiles wide and genuine, a captured moment of unguarded happiness. She picked it up and traced the outline of their faces with a trembling finger.

Their love had been a whirlwind, a passionate and intense journey that had swept them both off their feet. It was real, it was deep, and it was unbreakable. And yet, she realized that her health may cut their time together short. Painfully short.

The pressure of creating a perfect day, the weight of her health concerns, and the normal fears that came with such a life-changing commitment all collided within her as a silent tempest that nobody else could see or understand.

From afar, the city continued to pulse with life, indifferent to the quiet crisis unfolding within the walls of the opulent room. She needed to be strong for Jake and herself. But in that isolated moment, the floodgates opened, and she allowed herself the luxury of tears.

Why now? Why, when she was so close to having everything she had ever wanted, did the seeds of fear take root in her heart? Was it the impending marriage, the thought of facing an unknown future, or something else? Something deep within that whispered of times past and echoes of a life she could barely remember.

She wiped her tears away, knowing that soon, she would need to face Jake and look into his eyes and see the reflection of her own emotions. She needed to be the picture of happiness and anticipation, the bride he deserved. But in the quiet of her suite, with nightfall creeping over the skyline of Tokyo, Akiko allowed herself the freedom to be vulnerable, if only for a moment. In an uncharacteristic break from her calm, cool composure, she let herself go. She walked over to the table, flipped it over, and sent its contents flying. Delicate glassware broke on the unforgiving floor.

One floor below, Jake heard glass shattering and he looked up. In his heart, he knew it was Akiko. He fought the instinct to rush to her but gave in. He walked over and picked up his phone to call her. It just rings and goes to voicemail.

CHAPTER TWENTY-THREE
The Wedding

In the spacious hall of an upscale Tokyo hotel, filtered sunlight streamed through tall, arched windows and cast a soft glow on the rows of guests turned toward the back. The murmur of voices quieted to a hush as the music swelled—a classic, tender melody that seemed to echo the profound significance of the moment.

At the altar, Jake stood resplendent in a dark suit tailored to perfection. His hands were steady, but his heart beat a nervous rhythm against his ribcage. He took a deep breath and fixed his gaze on the double doors at the end of the long aisle.

Then, as if on cue, they opened.

Akiko appeared as a vision in white. Her gown flowed around her like a cascade of dreams woven into reality. Her dark hair was styled elegantly, a delicate tiara perched atop, and her face was alight with a radiant smile that seemed to outshine all the doubts and tears of the night before.

Flanked by two graceful women in colorful kimonos, their presence a nod to tradition amidst the modern setting, Akiko began her walk down the aisle. Each step was measured, yet there was a lightness to her that belied the gravity of her stride.

Jake's breath caught as their eyes locked, and in that glance, there was a silent exchange—a promise, a reassurance, and a declaration that no force in this world could sever the bond they were about to seal. He could see in her eyes the reflection of his soul and the acknowledgment of a journey that was their own—unique and unrepeatable.

The guests rose and their faces turned to follow Akiko's procession. They were enraptured by the beauty and solemnity of the bride. Whispers of admiration rustled like leaves in a gentle breeze, but Jake and Akiko were in a world of their own, surrounded by people yet alone together in their connection.

As Akiko reached the altar, her friends took their places to the side, and with tender grace, she stepped up to stand beside Jake. The officiant's welcome words were a distant sound as they took each other's hands, the touch a tangible reminder of the commitment they were making.

Their vows were spoken with conviction, each word a seal on their love and each promise a thread in the tapestry they would weave together in the years to come. Jake's voice was clear and strong. Akiko's sweet and unwavering. When they exchanged rings—simple, elegant bands of precious metal—it was more than a tradition; it was a symbol of eternal unity.

As they turned to face their friends and family, now joined as husband and wife, the applause and cheers filled the room, a crescendo of joy for the newlyweds. But amidst the celebration, it was the quiet understanding between Jake and Akiko that spoke volumes—a language of the heart that needed no words.

The wedding was not just a ceremony; it was the beginning of a new chapter, one they would write together with love as their guiding hand. And as they walked back down the aisle side by side, the future stretched out before them as a canvas waiting for the colors only they could bring to life.

CHAPTER TWENTY-FOUR

The Honeymoon

The Hawaiian sun was a gentle blaze in the clear sky. Its warmth was a comforting embrace for all the new beginnings. Azure waves lapped at the golden sands of a secluded beach where laughter blended with the symphony of the ocean. It was here that Jake and Akiko chose to celebrate their union away from the pulsating life of Tokyo, surrounded instead by the tranquil beauty of nature.

Jake was in his element, sporting board shorts with a vibrant pattern that matched the lively sparkle in his eyes. Akiko was radiant beside him. Her figure was adorned in a stylish bikini that complemented her natural grace. The two of them played in the ocean, splashing and teasing each other like a pair of carefree dolphins reveling in the freedom of the sea.

The water was a refreshing contrast to the sun's heat. It was invigorating and full of life. As they dove under the waves together, Akiko's health concerns were washed away, if only for the moment, by the saltwater's healing embrace. They swam out past where the waves broke, floated on the surface, and looked up at the sky as clouds drifted lazily by.

Now and then, Jake would glance over at Akiko to ensure she was at ease and to watch as the sun painted her skin with a golden hue. Akiko, for her part, seemed to have left every worry behind on the shores of Japan. Her laughter was a melody that danced over the water and her smile a beacon brighter than the sun-drenched sky above.

When they returned to the shore, they lounged on their beach towels, sipped from coconuts, and exchanged dreams of the future. Sometimes they spoke of travel, of destinations yet unexplored, and of simpler pleasures—quiet mornings shared, lazy Sundays, and the joy of finding each other amidst the chaos of life.

As the days passed, each sunset painted a masterpiece of colors across the horizon, and with each nightfall, the stars seemed to celebrate the love that Jake and Akiko shared. They would walk along the beach in the twilight, hands entwined, silhouettes against the canvas of dusk, the cool sand beneath their feet, and the whisper of the night wind in their ears.

The honeymoon was not just a respite but a reaffirmation of their vows and a testament to the power of love over adversity. It was a beginning not just of a marriage but of an adventure they had pledged to undertake together. With each passing day, their bonds grew stronger, their understanding deeper, and their commitment to each other unshakeable.

In this paradise, far from the complexities of their past lives, Jake and Akiko found a simple truth that they vowed to carry home with them: that no matter what the future held, they would face it together, with the same joy and passion they found in these tranquil Hawaiian waters.

The Hawaiian twilight cascaded its serene light over an elegant restaurant nestled by the sea. Tiki torches flickered like dancing spirits, and a gentle breeze carried the sweet fragrance of tropical flowers. Inside, the ambiance was a soft blend of island charm and understated luxury, the perfect setting for an intimate dinner for two.

Jake and Akiko sat at a secluded table with a view of the ocean. Its waves shimmered under the moon's tender gaze. They were dressed for the occasion; Jake in a crisp linen shirt and Akiko in a flowing dress that captured the island's spirit. The gentle clink of fine china and the soft conversations of other diners provided a gentle symphony as they savored their meal.

As they shared a dessert, a delicate concoction of local fruits and rich cream, Akiko's thoughts turned toward the future. "Jake, when we get back to Tokyo, I'd like you to meet with my attorneys. It's important to me that you're listed as my beneficiary for all of my assets."

Jake reached across the table and covered her hand with his own. His touch was warm and reassuring. "Akiko, I understand that's important, but let's not talk about attorneys and assets now. This time is about us, our love, and this beautiful beginning we're sharing."

He gave her hand a gentle squeeze, his eyes locking with hers and conveying a depth of sincerity. "When we return to Tokyo, we'll have all the time in the world to deal with that stuff. But here, now, I want us to focus on the sound of the waves, the beauty of the Hawaiian night, and the love that seems to resonate with every breeze that brushes against our skin."

Akiko's eyes softened and reflected the candlelight and the stars that peeked through the open-air venue. A small smile graced her lips as she withdrew her hand to reach for her glass of wine. "You're right, Jake. This moment is too precious to cloud with thoughts of what comes after."

Jake smiled gently. "I married you for you, not your assets. All I want is many, many years with you. I want you to outlive me."

She smiled softly. "Jake, that's not going to happen."

He looked away. The prospect of losing her was too painful to consider.

The conversation then drifted to lighter topics—tales of their child-hoods, their favorite memories from the past few days, and the adventures they still wanted to embark upon. They laughed and reminisced, and with each shared story, the bond between them grew stronger.

After the meal, they took a stroll along the beach, the sand cool beneath their feet and the rhythm of the sea a soothing backdrop to their silent communion. The world around them felt vast yet intimate, a paradox made possible by the island's enchanting atmosphere.

As they walked back to their hotel under the canvas of the starlit sky, Jake wrapped an arm around Akiko and pulled her close. They didn't need words to express what they felt; their shared silence was filled with understanding and affection.

Their honeymoon was more than a simple getaway; it was an affirmation of their commitment to each other, a time to celebrate their union, and a precious pause before they faced the complexities of life together. In these moments, they were reminded that while life's legalities would require attention, it was the love they carried in their hearts that was their truest treasure.

The sea's soothing song trailed off into the distance as Jake and Akiko retreated to the sanctuary of their hotel room. The room was aglow with the soft, warm light of bedside lamps that cast a serene ambiance and wrapped around them like a comforting embrace.

Slipping beneath the cool, crisp sheets of their bed, they nestled into the plush pillows, their bodies close, and hands entwined. The excitement of the day settled into a peaceful quiet as they faced each other. Their eyes spoke volumes in the hush of the night.

Akiko's gaze held Jake's with an intensity that seemed to capture the very essence of the stars outside. "Jake," she began, her voice a tender whisper, "now that we are married, there's a bond between us that transcends the physical. It's as eternal as the sky above us."

She moved closer, her head resting on his shoulder. "When my time in this world comes to an end, this bond will endure. And when you eventually join me, wherever that may be, we will be reconnected. Our souls are interwoven beyond the confines of life and death. You felt that and understood that when you visited those locations in Kyoto, right?"

Jake felt the weight of her words, profound and comforting. He lifted his hand to gently brush a strand of hair from her face. "Akiko, my love, I feel that connection deep within my soul. It's as if we were always meant to find each other, to unite in this lifetime and beyond. And yes, I felt that?"

They lay there in a tranquil embrace as the outside world melted away until there was nothing but the two of them, their shared heartbeat, and the promise of an eternal connection.

As sleep began to claim them, their last conscious thoughts were filled with a sense of peace. The fears and uncertainties of life seemed to lose their power in the face of their unwavering bond. They drifted off into dreams, comforted by the knowledge that their love had a depth that not even the finality of death could sever.

In the stillness of the Hawaiian night, two souls lay entwined, their love a testament to the timeless dance of destiny that had brought them together. They would cherish each other in this life and find each other again in the next.

CHAPTER TWENTY-FIVE

Hawaii to Tokyo

The Hawaiian sun dipped below the horizon and painted the sky with streaks of pink and orange as Jake and Akiko began to pack their belongings. Their suite, once a capsule of joyous seclusion, echoed with the rustle of clothes and the zip of suitcases closing. They worked in harmonious silence, each lost in thoughts of their shared memories and the life awaiting them back in Tokyo.

When they made a quick dash to the airport, the warm Hawaiian breeze tousled their hair for one final farewell. The airport was buzzing with activity, but within the flurry, Jake and Akiko were an island of calm as they moved steadily through the check-in process and security lines because they were still wrapped up in the cocoon of their honeymoon bliss.

Boarding the flight felt like a gentle nudge back to reality. As the plane soared into the twilight and left the idyllic shores behind, they settled into their seats. Akiko nestled her head on Jake's shoulder, and they both slipped into a restful sleep, the gentle hum of the engines a lullaby for their dreams.

Hours later, they were jolted awake by the landing gear touching down on Tokyo soil. The city greeted them with its familiar neon glow, a stark contrast to the tranquil beaches they had left behind. It was late, and the airport was quieter than usual. Their footsteps resonated in the emptiness as they made their way through the terminal.

Collecting their luggage, they hailed a taxi to take them back to their shared life in the city. The streets of Tokyo, a blend of shadows and light, whizzed by as they sat in reflective silence. Akiko's hand found Jake's, a silent expression of her ever-present support.

They arrived at their apartment building, and the doorman greeted them with a respectful bow. "Okaerinasai," he said, welcoming them home. Their apartment was just as they had left it, yet it now held a new significance as the first place they would live together as husband and wife.

As they unpacked, each item they stowed away seemed to be a symbolic act of weaving their lives together even more tightly. Clothes were folded into shared drawers, souvenirs placed on joint shelves, and two lives became even more entwined.

In the quiet of the night, with Tokyo's skyline shimmering beyond the window, they stood together and embraced the start of a new chapter. The excitement of their tropical retreat had given way to a serene anticipation of their future together.

As they finally settled into bed, the rhythm of the city lullaby eased them into a peaceful slumber. Tokyo might have been worlds apart from Hawaii but as long as they were together, any place felt like a paradise.

CHAPTER TWENTY-SIX
Home Sweet Home

Morning light streamed through the sheer curtains of their luxurious Tokyo apartment and cast a gentle glow across the room. Akiko's breaths were soft and even, the tranquil expression on her face a testament to the deep sleep she was enjoying. Jake stirred beside her but was careful to maintain the silence as he slipped out of bed. He dressed quietly in his gym attire, a simple gesture of consideration to let her rest a little longer.

With a last glance at Akiko's peaceful form, Jake stepped out into the brisk Tokyo morning. The air was cool and fresh, a stark contrast to the tropical warmth they had grown accustomed to in Hawaii. He set off at a steady pace, the rhythmic beat of his running shoes on the pavement marking the time as he wove through the waking city.

The streets of Tokyo were beginning to bustle with the early risers, and the hum of the city slowly rising in volume. Jake moved with the flow of the morning and felt the energy of the city invigorating him with every stride.

As his run came to an end, Jake found himself at the quaint local bakery they had discovered together during their first weeks in the apartment. The warm, inviting smell of freshly baked goods wafted out to greet him. He entered and was greeted by the cheerful bakery staff who recognized him. He selected an assortment of Akiko's favorite pastries—delicate, flaky treats filled with sweet bean paste and the lightest cream puffs dusted with powdered sugar.

With the pastries carefully wrapped, Jake made his way back to the apartment, his heart filled with anticipation at surprising Akiko with this small token of his love. He imagined her delight, the way her eyes would light up at the sight of the surprise breakfast, and how her smile would brighten the room more than the morning sun ever could.

Back at the apartment, he found Akiko still asleep. The pastries' enticing aroma was a secret enclosed in the paper bag. He set the table quietly and laid out the pastries with care alongside freshly brewed coffee to complete the morning feast.

As he turned to wake her, Akiko stirred and her eyes fluttered open to the new day. Jake sat at the edge of the bed, his hand gently brushing away a strand of hair from her face. "Good morning," he whispered, his voice filled with the warmth of his affection.

With a smile, Akiko sat up and wrapped the sheets around her as she took in the sight of Jake and the gentle morning light. The enticing smell had begun to fill the room. She followed him to the table and her eyes widened with delight at the spread before her.

"Surprise," Jake said, his smile mirroring hers. They sat together and let the comfort of their home envelop them as they enjoyed the pastries. Each bite was a sweet reminder of their new life together.

Home, they both knew, was not just a place, but wherever they were together, and as they shared this simple breakfast, their home felt like the sweetest place to be.

As the day unfolded, the easy rhythm of their morning routine gave way to the usual cadence of daily life. Akiko, ever so meticulous with her health, mentioned an appointment with her doctor. Jake, always the picture of concern, immediately offered to accompany her.

"No, love," Akiko said gently, touching his arm with a reassuring warmth. "You should enjoy your last day of vacation. I'll be fine—it's just a routine check-up."

The concern lingered in his eyes, but he nodded and respected her independence. After a tender kiss goodbye, Akiko stepped out, leaving Jake alone in the quiet of their apartment.

The hours stretched leisurely in front of him. It was an expanse of time he was not used to having. A plan formed in his mind—a nice dinner to welcome her back. A small celebration of normalcy after their idyllic escape to Hawaii. With the idea firmly planted, he left the apartment and headed to the local supermarket with a list of ingredients dancing in his head.

The aisles of the grocery store were a colorful array, brimming with fresh produce, fragrant herbs, and all manner of culinary possibilities. Jake moved through them with a sense of purpose and selected the freshest vegetables, the perfect cut of fish, and a bottle of her favorite wine. Each choice was an unspoken word in the love letter he planned to serve her for dinner.

With his shopping bags filled, he returned home. The quiet of the apartment greeted him once more. He set to work in the kitchen, and the clatter of pots and pans became a harmonious symphony to his focused task. Vegetables were chopped with care, the fish was seasoned just so, and the wine was set to chill. The kitchen was filled with the rich aromas of cooking and became a tangible sign of his devotion.

As the time for Akiko's return drew closer, the table was set with care. The ambiance of their dining room was warm and inviting. Jake lit candles and their flickering light cast a soft glow on the fine China and gleaming silverware. A vase of fresh flowers stood as a centerpiece. Their hues echoed the vibrancy of Tokyo life outside their serene haven.

He stood back, surveying his work with a satisfied nod, and imagined Akiko's smile and the joy in her eyes. It was these small moments, he realized, that wove the tapestry of their shared life—a tapestry rich with the threads of love and the vibrant colors of care and consideration.

When at last the sound of the door signaled Akiko's return, Jake's heart swelled. He greeted her with an embrace, a kiss, and the promise of a peaceful evening. As they sat down to the meal he had prepared, their conversation meandered from the mundane to dreams of their future. Laughter mingled with the clink of glasses.

The worries of the day, the doctor's visit, and the shadow of her health all fell away in the sanctuary they had created within these walls. Here, in their Tokyo home, the world outside could wait. Tonight, they had everything they needed.

CHAPTER TWENTY-SEVEN
Back to the Grind

The resounding chime of the elevator announced Jake's arrival at the Tokyo Gaming offices. As the doors slid open, he stepped out into the familiar hustle and bustle that had been his world before marriage, before Hawaii, and before everything had changed.

Colleagues spotted him and smiles broke across their faces. One by one, they approached and hearty congratulations echoed through the corridors. Each handshake, each pat on the back, and each exclamation of "Omedetou!" (Congratulations!) was a reminder of the new chapter he had just begun. They asked about the wedding, the honeymoon, and the life he had stepped into, but his answers were brief because his mind was elsewhere.

He settled into his chair and heard the familiar clack of the keyboard under his fingers as he tried to immerse himself in the codes and queries that comprised his work. But the pixels and lines of code morphed into memories—Akiko's laugh, the touch of her hand, and the way her eyes lit up under the Hawaiian sun. Each thought of her was a sweet echo that made the office walls seem to close in. The space around him felt too big and empty.

Through the glass walls of his office, the city stretched out—a vast tapestry of life and lights. It was back to the grind and back to reality, but his reality had shifted and was altered by the presence of Akiko in his life. Even as he toggled between screens, his work punctuated by the incessant buzz of office life, a part of him lingered with her, in the quiet comfort of their home, in the laughter that filled their rooms, and in the whisper of their shared secrets.

The clock ticked. It was a relentless reminder of the passing time, and he wondered how she was and what she was doing. Was she thinking of him too? A small smile played on his lips at the thought. He glanced at his phone, half-expecting, half-hoping for a message, but knew she too respected the sanctity of focus during work hours.

As the day wore on, the warmth of his colleagues' well-wishes mingled with his internal dialogue and became a gentle reassurance that despite the distance, Akiko was with him. Every code he wrote and every project he completed he did now with a new purpose—for her, for their future, and for the life they would build together.

When the hands of the clock finally signaled the end of the workday, he saved his work and shut down his computer. The anticipation of seeing Akiko again surged within him and it was like a tide that washed away the fatigue of the day. He grabbed his bag and made his way to the elevator, each step quickening with the promise of reunion. The grind was bearable because it led to her, and that made all the difference.

Exiting the corporate edifice that housed Tokyo Gaming, Jake paused. His day had been spent in a haze of work and wistful thoughts of Akiko. The hum of the city wrapped around him with its mix of distant conversations, the beeping of crosswalks, and the melodic chime of the closing elevator doors behind him. A floral shop across the street caught his eye—a beacon of color amidst the concrete gray.

He crossed and entered the shop. The scent of fresh blooms was a soothing balm. "Sumimasen," he called softly and began purchasing a bouquet of Akiko's favorites—delicate camellias with their lush petals and elegant simplicity. He imagined her surprise and her smile; it was worth every second lost in the commute home.

The journey back home was a blur. The closer he got the more his steps quickened with anticipation. But as he opened the door to their apartment, the vibrant bouquet dangled from his hand, and the scene that unfolded before him froze him in place.

Akiko lay motionless on the floor, a fallen angel amidst the serenity of their shared space.

"Akiko!" The flowers slipped from his grasp, petals scattering as he dropped to his knees beside her.

Her eyes fluttered open at his touch, her voice a mere whisper. "I'm okay," she insisted, even as her body betrayed her words. But Jake was already in motion and busy reviving her with words of love and the gentle pressure of his hands.

"I don't need a hospital," she murmured, her strength returning in increments. Despite her protest, he scooped her into his arms with ease. They were the same arms that had held her as they danced beneath Hawaiian stars.

He settled her into bed, tucked the covers around her, and pretended like they were a fortress against further harm. She clung to his hand, her grip a silent plea for him not to leave. So he stayed perched on the edge of their bed, still clad in his office attire.

The night grew old around them, stars trekked across the sky, and the city's heartbeat mellowed to the quiet hum of the early hours. But Jake did not move, except to ensure she was still breathing and still with him.

Her sleep was troubled and fitful. It was a stark contrast to the peaceful rest he wished for her. And so, he held her, a guardian against the encroaching night. The lines of his suit creased and his collar felt tight against his neck, but the discomfort was a small price to pay for her safety.

As dawn approached, its light caressing the horizon, Jake was a study in vigilance and love. The bouquet lay forgotten on the floor, its petals closed against the chill of the night, but in his heart, the promise of their love blossomed resolute and unwavering.

There, in the silence of the morning, with Akiko's gentle breathing a symphony to his ears, Jake made a silent vow. He would be her protector, her comfort, and her partner, in sickness and in health. This was the unspoken part of their vows, the depth of the "in sickness" clause that he embraced fully.

He didn't need to be anywhere else; he didn't want to be anywhere else. In the quiet surrender of the night, holding her, he understood the true weight of love. It was not just in the laughter and light but in the shadows and fears where love truly showed its relentless, unwavering face.

The sun rose in a hesitant crawl and diffused its gentle warmth through the gauzy curtains. Akiko stirred and her eyes met Jake's. They were filled with a quiet determination.

"I'll be fine, Jake. You should go to work," she whispered, her voice steadier than the flicker of fear in her eyes.

He searched her face and the familiar lines were etched with an unspoken plea for normalcy. "I can stay. I should stay," he countered, the protective instinct roaring in his veins.

But Akiko shook her head as a soft smile curved her lips. "I need you to go. I can't be the reason your world stops."

The conflict was evident in the set of his jaw and the hesitance in his eyes. Yet, the resolve in her voice was something he couldn't deny her.

Reluctantly, he agreed, so he showered swiftly and kept his movements mechanical. His suit felt like a costume or a uniform he donned to play a role when his heart was elsewhere.

He kissed her forehead and lingered longer than he meant to. "Call me—for any reason—and I'll be right back."

"I promise," she said, her hand gripping his with a strength that belied her frailty.

The apartment door closed with a soft click behind him and sealed her promise within. The outside world felt surreal. The normalcy of the morning commute was a stark contrast to the storm that raged within his heart.

Throughout the day, Jake's phone was a talisman he clutched. Every vibration and every chime had him lunging with a mix of fear and hope. But the call he dreaded, the call he needed, never came.

He was a man split in two—a diligent worker presenting charts and nodding through meetings, and a husband whose thoughts were ensnared by the image of Akiko, alone and vulnerable.

Time ticked by, each second a drumbeat echoing the rhythm of Akiko's promise. And as the sun arced its way across the sky, a testament to the enduring cycle of day and night, Jake held onto the hope that today, the promise would be enough.

Finally, the workday bled into the evening. His return was a rush of motion, the city a blur as he moved with a singular purpose. The apartment door swung open, and he found her there, a vision of resilience.

"How are you feeling?" he asked, the urgency in his voice softened by the relief washing over him.

"Better." She smiled, and for a moment, the shadow of fear lifted and was replaced by the enduring strength of their bond.

A wave of relief poured over Jake.

Akiko saw his relief and gently stroked his face. "How was work? Were you tired?"

Jake shook his head. "I wasn't. You were all I could think about. All day. But I am exhausted now."

Her smile reflected a tenderness and care he had never known. She gently stroked his face some more. "Let's order some food. You can get some sleep."

He agreed. "That sounds amazing. But let me take care of it. You rest."

A few hours passed and they had already eaten, showered, and gotten into bed. Jake was in a bathrobe as he lay on top of the covers next to Akiko, who was sleeping soundly under the covers. He still couldn't sleep. He was watching her breathe as he gently caressed her cheek.

CHAPTER TWENTY-EIGHT
Kamakura

The fading light of Friday evening found Jake turning the key in the lock and the familiar click closing out the work week. As he stepped into the soft warmth of their apartment, he found Akiko with her eyes carrying the sparkle of spontaneous adventure.

"Jake," she began, her voice a blend of excitement and hope. "Can we go to Kamakura for the weekend? I've been feeling good—really good—and I just... I want us to make memories there."

The seaside town of Kamakura, with its ancient temples and sweeping ocean views, was a place they had talked about visiting, and one of the many dreams penned on their ever-growing list. To see it now within reach sent a surge of happiness through him, especially after months of uncertainty regarding Akiko's health.

"Of course," Jake replied without a moment's hesitation. The word was less a reply and more a celebration. "Let's pack."

Together, they moved around the apartment with the comfortable efficiency of a couple deeply in tune with each other. Clothes were folded and placed into bags with whispers of fabric and essentials were gathered with the quiet anticipation of the journey ahead.

They worked in companionable silence, each lost in thoughts of the ocean's call and the serene escape that awaited them. Akiko's excitement was contagious; it settled in Jake's chest like a buoyant force that pushed away the lingering tendrils of worry that had become his unwanted companion.

In less than an hour, their weekend bags were packed. Their contents were a testament to their hopes. Swimsuits for the possibility of a sun-drenched beach, comfortable shoes for wandering along ancient paths, and, of course, a camera to capture moments that would soon become cherished memories.

As they zipped the bags closed, Akiko reached for Jake's hand. Her touch was a gentle anchor in the swift current of their lives. "Thank you," she said, her voice barely above a whisper, but her gratitude rang clear and true.

"For what?" Jake asked, his thumb brushing over her knuckles.

"For this," she gestured to the bags, to their home, and the invisible yet palpable tapestry of their life together. "For always saying 'yes' to life with me. For always being by my side."

Jake leaned in, his forehead resting against hers, his reply a promise carried on a breath. "Always."

The night settled in as a quiet prelude to the dawn of their adventure. Sleep came easily, and their dreams were a mingling of ancient shrines, ocean waves, and the shared heartbeat of anticipation.

Come morning, with the first rays of sunlight spilling through their window, Jake and Akiko set off to the train station on a journey not just of miles but of hearts finding joy in every step together.

The gentle sunlight of an early Saturday morning bathed the streets of Kamakura in a golden hue, which was an ancient town waking up to the soft sounds of the sea. Jake and Akiko walked hand in hand with their steps in sync and enjoyed the quiet harmony to the rhythm of the waking town.

Dressed in casual and comfortable clothes, Jake wore a soft cotton shirt that fluttered slightly in the seaside breeze. Akiko had her hair tied back in a loose ponytail and had donned a light summer dress that danced around her knees. Their attire was a silent nod to the unspoken agreement to leave behind the trappings of their busy Tokyo life, if only for a weekend.

The quiet was a welcome reprieve from the constant buzz of the city they were used to. Here, the air carried a different life—a blend of salt and pine and a freshness that seemed to cleanse the worries from one's soul with each breath. They passed by small shops just beginning to open. The owners were sweeping the entrances and offered smiles and morning greetings as they passed. The community spirit was as tangible as the cobblestones beneath their feet.

The casual wanderers ventured into a small, local café that promised the rich aroma of freshly ground coffee beans and the allure of traditional pastries. As they settled into a corner with their modest feast, the tranquility of the town wrapped around them like a comforting shawl. They were just two more faces among many. They were unremarkable, and for once, that was a blessing.

Their conversation was light and touched on the sights they wished to see: the Great Buddha that sat with timeless grace, the Tsurugaoka Hachimangu Shrine that had watched over countless seasons, and perhaps a stroll along the Yuigahama Beach where the waves whispered tales of old to those who would listen.

As they continued their exploration, the narrow lanes gave way to wider paths bordered by trees that swayed with the wisdom of the ages. The air carried the faint sounds of temple bells, a calling that seemed to draw them in with an almost magnetic pull. They followed the sound and eventually found themselves before the steps of a temple. Its gates were a silent welcome to all who sought its peace.

They took their time ascending the steps. Each one was a deliberate move away from the world they knew and drew them closer to something timeless. At the top, they paused, not just to catch their breath, but to let the serenity of the place sink into their bones.

Akiko's hand tightened around Jake's as a wordless expression of contentment. They didn't need to speak to know that they were both feeling the same thing—a deep connection to the world and each other.

The day stretched out before them as hours unclaimed and waiting to be filled with the simple joy of being together in a place that felt suspended between the earth and the sky. Kamakura, with its blend of nature and nurture, history and the present, was the perfect backdrop for their love story to continue unfolding, one quiet, shared moment at a time.

The morning light filtered through the blinds and cast a soft glow on the room. Despite the allure of Kamakura waiting outside, Jake and Akiko allowed themselves the luxury of sleeping in. The soft sheets and the quiet hum of the seaside air lulled them into a contented slumber. When they did wake, it was past the rush of morning and into a lazy, sun-drenched late start.

Akiko stretched gracefully, her movements cat-like and languid and her eyes bright with a secret excitement. When she whispered to Jake, her voice was still thick with sleep. "There's a place I want to show you. It's a part of Kamakura that not many tourists know about."

Intrigued, Jake followed her lead as they dressed in comfortable attire suitable for a hike. Akiko seemed to know exactly where she was going. Her steps were sure and excited as they left the beaten path and started up into the hills. The air grew cooler as they ascended and the scent of the sea mingled with the earthy fragrance of damp moss and leaves.

The path was less maintained here. It was overgrown in parts with the vibrant green of nature reclaiming its territory. It was a climb that required a bit more effort and a bit more care with each step, but the seclusion of the path lent a private air to their journey. Birds called out in high trills, and somewhere in the distance, the sound of water suggested a hidden stream or waterfall.

Finally, they arrived at a small temple nestled in the cradle of the hills. It was a humble structure that was made of aged wood that had seen many seasons with paper lanterns that fluttered gently in the breeze. The temple exuded a sense of timeless solitude and its presence was a quiet testament to the spiritual history of the place.

Beyond the temple was a shrine that was even more secluded and surrounded by towering trees that seemed to stand guard. The shrine was a simple affair and had a small torii gate at the entrance that marked the transition from the mundane to the sacred.

They paused before the gate, and Akiko took a deep breath as her eyes closed for a moment in reverence. When she stepped through, Jake felt as if they were entering another world. He was sure he had been here before. The atmosphere was thick with the weight of unspoken prayers and dreams left by those who had come before.

Akiko's voice was soft, almost reverent. "This shrine is someplace we have visited before. A long, long, time ago. Can you feel it?"

Jake nodded yes. He definitely could feel it. They approached the shrine together, the gravel underfoot crunching in the quiet. Akiko showed Jake how to purify their hands at the chozuya and they offered prayers by the clapping of their hands briefly and breaking the silence. They stood side by side with their heads bowed and hands pressed together in a moment of shared spirituality. As she talked him through the process, he nodded solemnly, as he already knew what she would say next.

Afterward, they sat on the edge of a nearby wooden bench with the tranquility of the shrine enveloping them. Akiko rested her head on Jake's shoulder and her hand found his. Their fingers interlaced with ease. Here, in the embrace of the Kamakura Hills with the sacredness of the shrine as their witness, they found a new depth to their connection. It transcended the physical and touched the soul.

Akiko looked deeply into Jake's eyes. "In this place, the bridge between past and present is incredibly short. If you close your eyes and meditate, you can feel the people who have been here and the things that took place here. Do you understand that?"

He nodded his head.

Slightly hesitant, Akiko asked, "Would you like to try it?"

Jake nodded his head.

She smiled slightly and took his hand. "Let's close our eyes and just relax. Completely clear your thoughts."

The scene changed. They were in the same location and the same temple, but it was hundreds of years earlier. Jake was dressed in the elegant attire of a Tokugawa-era Samurai and was standing watch over the grounds. His eyes were filled with steely seriousness.

Akiko emerged from the tunnel that joined the temple to the town below. She was the picture of refined elegance. She made her way over to a small, bright red bridge and walked out to the middle. As she peered down into the koi pond below, she looked up.

Her eyes met with Jake's.

Their moment was interrupted by the shout of a shopkeeper who was walking toward Akiko. He was visibly angry and shouting and gesturing. He was upset that Akiko's father was increasing the taxes he needed to pay to operate his business.

Jake wasted no time. He hurried onto the path and got between the angry shopkeeper and Akiko. Jake angrily barked, "Take one more step, and I will cut you down."

The man is shocked, and he stops. He glared at Jake. Jake stares back with a deadly intensity in his eyes. The man backed away and began to point and shout at Akiko., "Tell your father I will never stand for this. I will find him and I will make him pay."

Jake stepped forward and in one motion, grabbed the man by his hair and dragged him to the ground. In a sudden flash of violence, he removed his sword and his katana began slicing through the air with breathtaking swiftness and accuracy.

The man's head is separated from his body and it rolls onto the ground. A massive pool of crimson blood instantly pooled beside the body of the man who was shouting threats and insults at Akiko mere moments before.

Akiko staresdin awe at Jake. Jake remained expressionless. After a long moment, Jake respectfully bowed to Akiko.

Now, we return to the present day with Jake and Akiko sitting on the bench on the ancient temple grounds. Jake's eyes flashed open and he looked around. Akiko's eyes calmly moved over to scan Jake's expression. Jake breathed deeply as he asked, "We knew each other?"

Akiko gave him a nod and a subdued smile. "Yes, we did."

An uneasy quiet settled over the two. Jake looked to Akiko."Did I kill somebody? Just like that?"

Akiko nodded. "To protect me. And my father."

Jake tried to process this while Akiko continued, "This was our first life together. This is how we first met."

Jake looked at Akiko. "So after this, we were...together?"

Akiko nodded. A sadness comes over her face. "Yes."

"I feel like there is more to this. Something you're not telling me." Jake pressed.

Again Akiko nodded. "Our time together was very short. But very intense. It bonded us for all of eternity."

The two sat on the bench. The beauty of the temple grounds was overshadowed by this revelation. Akiko took Jake's hand.

"Let's leave." Jake looked at her, "Can we see... The next part?"

He wanted to go back and see more. Akiko shook her head and appeared visibly shaken. "No, let's leave."

Jake was curious, but he trusted her, so he nodded his head. Together they stood up to leave. The suddenness and urgency of her request to leave was puzzling, however.

They walked through the grounds and back to the tunnel where Akiko's father emerged hundreds of years before. She walked to the tunnel and entered without looking back. Jake was looking back at the grounds with a mix of disbelief and awe on his face.

CHAPTER TWENTY-NINE
Homecoming

Jake and Akiko, walked hand in hand down a bustling side street of the ancient town. Although their hands were joined, they were in two different places entirely. Akiko was focused on taking Jake through Kamakura and showing him what he needed to see. Jake was in awe as he soaked in the atmosphere. Everywhere he looked, he felt a sense of deja vu to a life he lived hundreds of years ago. Akiko pointed to a small restaurant up on an embankment that was shrouded in lush trees.

"We are here. This is the one."

They walked up the embankment and entered the restaurant.

There were a few other diners in the small, historic restaurant, but Jake and Akiko were locked in an intimate conversation.

Jake felt a shift in Akiko. "You okay?"

She smiled sweetly. "Never better. Are you?"

He nodded. "Today was...a lot."

She nodded.

Jake continued, "When I asked to go back and see more...it felt like I upset you. Are you okay?"

She nodded. "It wasn't you. But yes, it was upsetting."

Jake processed this before Akiko continued. "Do you want to know the full story?"

Jake contemplated carefully before answering. "Yes. I really do."

Akiko gathered her composure. As she prepared to bring Jake up to speed, the server appeared with their food. Akiko and Jake both look startled. The server placed their food on the table with a smile. Jake and Akiko both nodded in appreciation before Akiko continued.

"It was a really difficult time, Jake. You did your duty. You protected my family and me." She looks down.

Jake waited patiently.

A long moment passed and she continued, "The man you killed. He was a prominent shopkeeper. He had deep Yakuza ties and political ties. Ending his life hurt them financially."

Jake listened intently.

Akiko soldiered on. "It started a chain of events. A bad chain of events. They killed Yuki, my sister. She was only ten. They did it to send a message and get revenge."

Jake took her hand. "I'm so sorry, Akiko."

She shook her head. "He was a despicable, violent, and horrible man. The town called you a hero. Privately. But after my sister was killed, my father took his own life. He could not overcome his grief. It was a very dark time."

Jake interrupted and pulled his hand back. "I am so sorry."

She shook her head. "So you did what you did best. You were an incredible and very brave warrior. You took revenge. You didn't just kill those responsible, you slaughtered them. You became a hero in the town. You freed them from years of terror."

Jake looked around the restaurant. His mind raced with questions. "So I?.."

She held her hand up. She needed to finish. "Your Daimyo, your boss, he bowed to pressure and ordered you to commit seppuku. And you did."

Jake was dumbfounded. Akiko took Jake's hand and looked into his eyes with a deep passion that had burned for centuries. "I was already in love with you. You only did what you did for me and my family. Your ceremony took place on the most beautiful day of the year. The cherry blossoms were in full bloom. A gentle breeze was blowing them through the air, and they were falling on the ground like snow. I remember watching you. You were so brave. So dignified. You were a role model not just to your Lord, but to the whole town. The whole region. When you...did it...I resolved that I would end my own life too. So we could be together in our next life. And that night, I did.

Jake's eyes softened and tears welled up in his eyes.

CHAPTER THIRTY

Promises

Jake and Akiko were nestled into a private cabin on the high-speed train that was taking them back to Tokyo. They were both tired, but neither could sleep. Akiko was holding Jake's hand as they both looked out the window at the blur of lights passing by at ridiculously high speed. Akiko tugged on Jake's hand and their eyes locked.

"Promise me something?" She asked. "When my time comes to an end in this life. I want you to continue on. I want you to live a long full life. Promise me that?"

He processed this for a moment and nodded. She is not convinced, and deep down, neither is he.

Minutes passed. The hum of the high-speed train was the only sound in the quiet cabin. Jake broke the silence. "I can't promise you that."

Her eyes lit up with passion and intensity, and there was a tinge of anger in her voice. "You must. I will wait for you for all of eternity if I have to."

He shook his head. "Fuck that. I love you. I always have. Even before I met you. My friends and family said I was crazy to take a job and move to Japan. I knew I had to. I just somehow knew I had to. Now that I have you, it all makes sense. My life was empty and meaningless until that night outside of the office."

"Promise me. I need you to promise me." she pleaded. She peered not into his eyes but into his soul.

His expression softened. He can tell how much this meant to her. Reluctantly, he nodded and said, "I promise."

Satisfied, she slipped back into her position with her head nestled on Jake's shoulder, still holding his hand. Jake peered out the window, lost in thought.

CHAPTER THIRTY-ONE
Three Months Later

Three months had flown by in a whirlwind of change and adaptation for Jake. The once familiar layout of the Tokyo Gaming office had taken on a new dimension in his life, and it was a testament to his hard work and dedication. Now, as a Director in the marketing department, his days were filled with a flurry of activity and decision-making, which was a far cry from the cubicle he once called his second home.

His new office, which was located on the executive suite floor, was a spacious, well-lit corner room with a stunning view of the Tokyo skyline. The walls were adorned with artwork that spoke of his love for both the traditional and the modern and was a reflection of his journey in Japan. A large, polished desk dominated the room, and on it sat a photo framed of him and Akiko, smiling and radiant on their wedding day.

The door to his office was perpetually ajar. It was a silent invitation for collaboration and open communication. Colleagues, both old and new, frequently popped in to share ideas or seek guidance. Each visitor brought with them a spark of creativity, a challenge to be met, or a problem to be solved, which made every day a dynamic experience.

As Jake reviewed the latest campaign proposals, there was a soft knock on the door. "Come in," he called, without looking up.

A young team member, Mika, stepped in hesitantly, clutching a folder to her chest. "Jake-san, I have some ideas for the new product launch. Could you please take a look?"

Jake nodded and gestured to the chair across from him. "Of course, Mika. Let's hear them."

She laid out her concepts with an infectious eagerness. Jake listened attentively by nodding along, asking questions, and offering suggestions. The exchange was a dance of creativity and strategy and each idea was a step toward a shared goal. As Mika stood to leave, she looked at Jake with a seductive gleam in her eye. "Jake-san, I was planning to go out with friends tonight. If you don't have plans, would you like to join us for a drink? We will be at Nirvana in Shinjuku?"

Jake gave Mika a polite smile. "Ah, thank you, but I already have plans."

Mika continued, "I hope that wasn't rude, but I told all of my friends about you. You really make work fun. They all want to meet you. They are all very jealous of me."

Jake grinned. "You give me way too much credit, but thank you, Mika. That's very kind of you."

Mika took a piece of paper and put it on his desk. Her name and number were already written on it. "If you change your mind, please text me. It's an open invite."

Jake smiled with a forced appreciation. He took the paper and put it in his pocket. She was visibly infatuated with Jake, and he didn't want to hurt her feelings or curb her professional ambitions.

As the day progressed, more colleagues came and went and each interaction reinforced Jake's belief in the power of teamwork and diverse perspectives. The clock hands moved steadily and eventually marked the passage of a productive day.

In the quiet moments between meetings, Jake's thoughts drifted to

Akiko. He wondered how she was spending her day and hoped she was taking it easy and looking after her health. His phone suddenly buzzed with a message from her. It was a simple heart emoji, but it still brought a smile to his face. It was their little way of staying connected—a digital heartbeat that pulsed with love.

The sun began its descent and soon cast long shadows across the room. Jake leaned back in his chair to take a moment to appreciate the journey that had brought him here. From the bustling streets of Los Angeles to the vibrant heart of Tokyo, his life had been a tapestry of unexpected turns and challenges.

His gaze fell on the photo of him and Akiko. It served as a reminder of the strength and support that lay waiting for him at home. With a contented sigh, he began to tidy his desk, wrapping up another day at the office. Home was calling, and with it, the promise of a peaceful evening with the woman who was his anchor in the ever-changing tides of life.

The journey home felt longer for Jake because his mind was preoccupied with thoughts of Akiko. He quickened his pace, his footsteps echoing on the pavement under the bustling Tokyo lights. The familiar streets, once brimming with intrigue, now only served as a pathway leading him back to her.

Upon arriving at their apartment, a sense of quiet greeted him. It was a stark contrast to the lively energy of the office. The apartment was dimly lit, and the only light emanated from the bedroom. A tinge of concern nipped at him as he removed his shoes and made his way silently inside.

As he entered the bedroom, he found Akiko lying in bed, her features drawn and pale under the soft glow of the bedside lamp. She attempted a weak smile as he approached, but it didn't quite reach her eyes.

"Hey, how are you feeling?" Jake asked gently. He sat on the edge of the bed and reached for her hand.

"Not great," she admitted softly, her voice barely above a whisper. "I've been in bed all day. I didn't want to worry you."

Jake's heart clenched at her words. He brushed a stray lock of hair from her forehead and kept his touch tender. "You should have called me. I would have come home right away."

She squeezed his hand in silent appreciation for his concern. "I know, but you had that big meeting today. I didn't want to disturb."

He leaned down and planted a soft kiss on her forehead. "You're more important than any meeting, Akiko. You know that."

Her eyes fluttered closed at his touch and a small sigh escaped her lips. Jake could feel the feverish warmth of her skin and a silent alarm raised his worry.

"Let me make you some soup or something light," he offered, standing up. "And I'll call Dr. Saito, just to check in."

Akiko nodded. Her energy was spent. Jake moved around the apartment with quiet efficiency and began preparing a simple broth. The comforting aroma filled the space. After setting her up with the soup and ensuring she ate a little, he stepped out to make the call.

Dr. Saito listened with concern and advised them to monitor Akiko's condition and to bring her in if there was no improvement. Jake thanked her, and his mind was already racing through the necessary steps to care for Akiko.

Returning to the bedroom, he found Akiko dozing. The soup was barely touched. He set the bowl aside and slipped into bed beside her, his arm gently encircling her. His presence was a silent vow and a promise to weather any storm together.

The night passed in quiet vigil. Jake stayed awake watching over her. His mind oscillated between worry and the memories of their brighter days. Akiko's breathing, though uneven, was a constant reminder of the fragility and strength of life.

At around 1 a.m., Akiko stirred restlessly. Her eyes fluttered open to meet Jake's concerned gaze. A faint smile graced her lips, and it was a shadow of her usual vibrant self. "Jake, could you do something for me?" she asked, her voice weak but filled with a longing for a taste of normalcy.

"Anything," Jake replied, his eyes searching hers for any sign of discomfort.

"There's this shop in Shinjuku, remember? They have those little treats I love so much. Could you...would you mind?" Her request hung in the air as a gentle plea for a piece of the world outside their quiet room.

Understanding the unspoken desire behind her words, Jake nodded. "Of course. I'll be back before you know it." He quickly dressed and headed out into the night. The streets of Tokyo were eerily quiet at this late hour.

The city, a different world under the moon's watch, was more subdued but still alive with its nocturnal rhythm. He made his way to Shinjuku. The lights of the district cut through the darkness and led him to the shop Akiko cherished.

As he was about to head back with Akiko's treats, a familiar voice called out his name. Turning, he saw Mika with a group of friends. Her cheeks were flushed with the merriment of the night and her laughter was free and easy in the quiet street.

"Jake-san! You came!" she exclaimed, slightly unsteady on her feet.

Jake hesitated. The bag of treats in his hand was a reminder of his purpose. "I should get back to my wife," he explained. His concern for his wife colored his tone.

Mika, in her slightly inebriated state, pouted playfully. "Just one drink. Come on! It's not every day we get to hang out outside of work. Plus, I told all of my friends you were coming!" Mika's friends, all young, pretty, and well-dressed, smiled playfully at him.

"Thanks for the offer, Mika, but Akiko's not doing well. I need to get back to her," Jake replied, his voice firm yet polite.

Mika's expression softened into a slight pout of disappointment and flirtation. "Your wife is the luckiest woman on earth. I would not let you out of my sight if you were mine. Please tell her I hope she feels better though?"

"I won't tell her the first part, but I will tell her you said to feel better. Thank you, Mika. Have a good night, and stay safe," Jake said with a friendly nod, turning to leave.

The walk back was faster, and his steps were spurred by the thought of Akiko waiting for him. The night air felt cooler now, which was a sharp contrast to the warmth he anticipated in their home.

Upon his return, he found Akiko awake. Her eyes lit up at the sight of the treats. "You have no idea how much I love you, Jake," she murmured. A genuine smile spread across her face.

He grinned. "I think you make that abundantly clear."

As they shared the treats, the clock ticked in the background. The simplicity of the moment filled Jake with an overwhelming sense of gratitude. Life had its complexities and its unexpected turns, but it was moments like these - small, intimate, and filled with love - that made everything worthwhile. He felt a sense of guilt for spending even thirty seconds talking with Mika and her friends.

Akiko, oblivious to Mika's seductive pleas, sat up in bed and thoroughly enjoyed the treats while Jake changed back into his pajamas.

Chapter Thirty-Two
Endings and Beginnings

The Tokyo Gaming office buzzed with its usual frenzy of activity, but for Jake, time seemed to move at a different pace. Seated in his executive office, his gaze wandered past the computer screen to the world outside the window—a sprawling cityscape that held so many memories.

His mind drifted back to the night he had first met Akiko outside this very building. It had been raining—a downpour that seemed to wash the entire city clean. He remembered how she had looked under the building's overhang, elegant and composed, yet vulnerable in the storm. And how, with a simple act of sharing his umbrella, their lives had become irreversibly intertwined.

Lost in these reflections, the ringing of his office phone jolted him back to the present. It was a call he had been dreading, yet one he knew was inevitable. Dr. Saito's voice, usually so calm and measured, carried a weight that immediately set Jake's heart racing.

"Jake-san, it's Akiko," the doctor began, the words careful and deliberate. "I'm afraid her condition has worsened significantly. We've done all we can, but it might be time to prepare yourself...."

The words hit Jake like a physical blow and each syllable was a heavy weight that threatened to crush him. He gripped the phone tighter as if holding on to it could somehow change the reality of Dr. Saito's message.

"But she's been doing better. Her fever has been improving?" Jake protested weakly, his voice a mixture of hope and despair.

"I understand this is difficult, Jake-san," Dr. Saito continued, her voice tinged with empathy. "These fluctuations can happen. But the signs are clear. It might be best to spend as much time with her as possible."

The finality in her words was unmistakable and was a stark reminder of the cruel unpredictability of life. Jake felt a numbness spread through him and it became a protective shell against the pain that threatened to overwhelm him.

"Thank you, Dr. Saito," he managed to say, his voice barely above a whisper. He hung up the phone slowly, his movements robotic.

The office, his colleagues, the endless stream of emails and meetings—all of it suddenly seemed inconsequential. There was only one thing that mattered now: Akiko.

He stood up, his chair rolling back with a soft thud. Without a word to anyone, he grabbed his coat and left the office. The corridors were a blur, and the elevator descent was an agonizingly slow journey to the ground floor.

Stepping out into the streets of Tokyo, Jake barely noticed the city's vibrant life around him. His steps were automatic and led him home to Akiko and to their shared sanctuary where joy and sorrow had danced in equal measure.

The apartment door opened to a silence that was louder than any sound. Akiko was there. She appeared weaker, yet still as beautiful as the night they met. Their eyes met and a thousand words passed between them in a single glance.

He approached her, but his steps were hesitant. Each one was a reluctant acceptance of the reality they now faced. They embraced and in that embrace was the entirety of their journey—a tapestry of love, laughter, tears, and now, an impending goodbye.

As they held each other, the world outside faded away and left only the truth of their moment. A truth that was as beautiful as it was heartbreaking.

In the quiet of their apartment, Akiko's voice, though frail, carried a firm resolve. "Jake, could you do something for me?" Her eyes, reflecting a mix of sadness and love, met his. "Could you go to Shinjuku and get those treats we both love? I want us to enjoy them together... one last time."

Jake's heart ached at her request. It was a simple desire laden with unspoken finality. The thought of leaving her side, even for a moment, tore at him. But he saw in her eyes a longing for a semblance of normalcy, and a desire to savor a shared joy amid their sorrow.

"Of course, Akiko," he replied, his voice thick with emotion. He leaned down, kissed her forehead gently, and memorized the feel of her skin under his lips.

With a heavy heart, Jake left the apartment. The streets of Tokyo, usually a backdrop to his daily life, now felt distant, as if he were moving through a dream. The vibrant energy of Shinjuku, the buzz of the crowd, the neon glow—it all seemed surreal, a stark contrast to the quiet, poignant scene he had left behind.

He arrived at the familiar shop, and the sight of it brought a bittersweet pang. The treats that had once been a symbol of shared happiness now felt like a tender farewell. He made the purchase, with tears filling his eyes. Each movement was mechanical and his mind was racing back to Akiko.

Returning home, he found that he was too late.

The moment he entered their apartment everything felt different. The energy of their shared love was absent. The energy that filled the room wasn't dread. It was just empty. An emptiness that he had never before felt. Jake knew in his heart that he was too late. Tears streamed down his face as he walked over to her and touched her face. She was ice cold.

He placed the bag of treats down on the nightstand beside her and crawled into bed next to her. He looked at her face, angelic even in death. Her eyes were closed, her expression the same gentle smile that won his heart. He softly kissed her cheek and brushed the hair off of her forehead.

Jake sat up and stared at Akiko's face. He knows that this was one of the last times he would ever see her. He felt so alone. So lost. His mind raced through the memories of the times they shared and the dreams they once held so close. He knew this moment would come, but he always denied it – the prospect was simply too painful to acknowledge. Here he sits, imagining what life would be like without her. His memory flashed back to the moment she looked into his eyes and asked him, pleaded with him, to live his life after she was gone. Tears welled up in Jake's eyes as he gently stroked her face.

Jake got up from the bed and looked around the place they once shared. He made his way into the bathroom and returned moments later, a full bottle of prescription strength sleeping pills they had just picked up resting in his hands. Jake sat at their small desk beside the bed, picked up a pad, and started writing. There were so many things he needed to explain to his friends and family. Fighting back tears, he wrote – each line sharing the love story they had lived. As he sat, he thought back to something he once heard: "It is better to have loved and lost, than to have never loved at all," and it brought a smile to his face.

His note was complete. He stared at the pad now sitting on the desk. The people that he loved, and that loved him, would they understand? Could they forgive him? He didn't know. Minutes passed as he sat in contemplation. Standing from the desk, he took the bottle of pills and removed the cap. He took a handful of pills and swallowed them. Climbing back into bed, he nuzzled up close to her. In her ear, he whispered, "I love you. In this life and every other." He gently stroked her cheek as he drifted off into a deep sleep.

THE END

www.ingramcontent.com/pod-product-compliance
Lightning Source LLC
Chambersburg PA
CBHW071431130726
47997CB00006B/2044